JIM REAPER

JIM REAPER
Son of Grim

Rachel
Delahaye

Illustrations by
Jamie Littler

Piccadilly
PRESS

First published in Great Britain in 2016 by
PICCADILLY PRESS
80–81 Wimpole St, London W1G 9RE
www.piccadillypress.co.uk

A CIP catalogue record for this book
is available from the British Library.

ISBN: 978-1-84812-487-5
also available as an ebook

1

Typeset by Palimpsest Book Production Limited,
Falkirk, Stirlingshire
Printed and bound by Clays Ltd, St Ives Plc

Piccadilly Press is an imprint of Bonnier Publishing Fiction,
a Bonnier Publishing company
www.bonnierpublishingfiction.co.uk
www.bonnierpublishing.co.uk

For Matilda and Ben, whom I love to death

Where it Started to Get Weird . . .

'Blood?' Will rasped. 'He just said *blood*!'

I grabbed the phone and held it against my ear. The raspy voice fizzed down the old telephone line.

'. . . *You haven't done blood before, I know that. But you can do it, and I have no doubt you're the best man for the job. I'm offering you a promotion. A pay rise. Will you think about it?*'

It was my dad's boss! He thought he was talking to Dad, and he was waiting for an answer!

'Yes,' I replied in my gruffest Dad voice, before putting the phone down quickly.

I looked at Will with alarm. His eyes goggled back at me.

'You were right, Will,' I nodded. 'He said blood. He wants Dad to take a job involving blood.'

'Flippin' pancakes! Flippin' nutty pancakes, Jim!' he spluttered.

I couldn't blame Will for flipping out. Dad wasn't a surgeon or a forensic scientist or a paramedic. He was an accountant. Accountants don't usually do bloody things, apart from bloody maths. And if there's one thing I know for sure about Dad, it's that he's scared of blood. Faints at the sight of it. Once I grazed my knee and he was unconscious for twenty minutes.

There had to be a straightforward explanation.

'"Blood" could be a tricky mathematics formula,' Will said. 'Maybe it stands for Binding Large Overcomplicated Odious Digits.'

'Or it could be a surname,' I said brightly. 'Yes, that's probably it.'

The phone rang again – a high-pitched clattering, like marbles rattling in a tin. Without thinking, Will picked up the receiver again. He panicked and flapped his free hand at me. Gently, I took the receiver from him and held it against my ear.

'*Oh, and another thing. Just checking you'll be at the boardroom meeting at seven p.m. on Thursday?*'

'Er, yes,' I gruffed again.

'Excellent, excellent. See you then.'

And that was the end of that. Although, well, it wasn't.

Chapter 1

But let's go right back to the beginning. Before I discovered something that would turn my life inside out and upside down.

You might have heard about how the universe began with the Big Bang?

Well, the universe as I knew it was about to end. With a Bazoom!.

You probably never had the chance to set eyes on a Bazoom! so let me tell you a bit about it. The Bazoom! (exclamation mark included) was a scooter big enough to carry a rider and a passenger, and it had an electric gadget behind the back wheels called a pop-boost. One press of the button on the handlebars and that pop-boost gave you a split-second blast of speed. It was totally awesome.

When it first appeared in Scoots, the scooter shop, everyone drooled over it like it was made of sugar and talked about it non-stop. I don't think parents knew the real meaning of 'pester-power' before the Bazoom! came along. For me, it was just another one of those things I'd be happy to daydream about – like a racing car or a flying suit with fully functioning detachable wings. Bazoom!s cost hundreds of pounds. They were also limited edition (which means only a few were ever made) – so when Scoots ran out, there'd be no more. Nope, I wasn't going to get my guts in a twist over owning a Bazoom!. There were more important things in life. Or so I thought . . .

On Mondays I go back to Will Maggot's house after school because Dad's at work, Mum's at yoga and Hetty, my sister, does drama club. It's fine by me for lots of reasons:

1. Will's my best friend
2. Will's mum makes normal, delicious food, and
3. Will has a sister, Fiona, who has these green eyes and dimples and, well, she's just a little bit awesome (but don't tell anyone I said that).

This Monday the three of us – me, Will and Fiona – wheeled our scooters up the big hill on the way home together. I was telling Will about the dark patch on our roof I'd been investigating and how I thought it could have something to do with alien landings. Fiona walked two steps ahead and wore headphones so she didn't have to listen to our stupid conversations (her words), which was a bit upsetting. But not as upsetting as the presence of Jeremy Flowers. He had trailed us all the way from school, shouting rude things and trying to get our attention.

'Oi, oi!' he called from the other side of the road. 'Maggot and Wimple – one worm, one simple!'

We ignored him but Jeremy laughed anyway. His laugh is nasty, like a throaty cough, and he opens his mouth really wide, which is revolting because he has bright red gums and loads of teeth that go in different directions. Will says his mouth looks like a hookworm's.

I've never seen a hookworm and I don't think I ever want to.

'Oi! Maggot!' he shouted. 'With a face like yours who needs enemies?'

'Just keep walking,' I told Will.

'How's your snail collection?' Jeremy shouted. 'Or do you collect STAMPS now?' He stamped his foot and hooted hysterically (there's a story behind that – I'll tell you later).

'Leave us alone,' I said.

'Oh yeah, want to come here and say that, Simple Wimple?'

Jeremy dropped his bag at his feet and held his arms out. He definitely wasn't asking for a hug. By the look on his snarled face, he was getting ready to do something nasty, so I was relieved when Will ran forward and tugged Fiona's jacket. It was definitely Fiona-intervention time. Fiona took off her headphones, rolled her eyes and walked across the road. She said something we couldn't hear and poked Jeremy in the chest a couple of times until he picked up his bag and backed away looking flustered. As he ran away, Fiona dusted her hands, as calm as if she'd just posted a letter. Awesome. She then checked her mobile phone and her face sprouted dimples.

'Babysitting duty is officially over. Later, losers,' Fiona grinned. She folded up her scooter and ran up the road.

'Why is Fiona running?' I asked Will. She usually moved slowly, like a stalking tiger, but right now she was all cheetah and disappearing fast into the distance.

'Her special delivery has probably arrived.'

I watched as Fiona melted into a dot at the end of the road. Then a loud *pop* broke the spell. It was a Bazoom! pop-boosting right past us, shiny and red like a sucked boiled sweet. A red Bazoom! . . . Double awesome. I sighed.

'You sighed aloud,' said Will, staring at me as if I'd been rude.

'Sighing is an aloud thing,' I said. 'You can always hear a sigh.'

'Sighing should be personal,' Will disagreed. 'You were making it very public.'

We turned into Will's road. It's a terraced street, the kind where houses and all their families are squished together side by side and everyone is really friendly.

'Do you want to know what I was sighing about?' I asked.

'Well, a sigh suggests there are no words to explain how you're feeling. So there's no point.'

'The Bazoom!,' I said, ignoring him. 'Did you see it? The red one that went past? It was amazing. Totally sigh-some.'

'Oh that,' said Will disinterestedly. 'Fiona's just bought one. That's her special delivery.'

'What? Why didn't you tell me?'

'You didn't ask,' Will said, pulling a 'der!' face.

When we got to Will's house, there, in the front garden, was a metallic green scooter, big and mean like a praying mantis. My mouth dropped open. I couldn't even sigh.

'Come on,' Will said. 'Fiona will kill you if she sees you breathing on it.'

I was going to explain that you can't see breathing, but Will had already opened the door.

'Come in, boys!' Will's mum shouted. She was listening to loud pop music. Will's mum is pop crazy. She carries her little radio round the house with her so she can dance wherever she is. She's usually in the kitchen – it's where she cooks, dances and hangs washing on metal racks. There's a TV in there too, which my mum would never allow in our house.

When we went in, the top half of Will's mum was buried in the fridge-freezer but she was still managing to dance with her bottom half, which stuck out at a funny angle. She shuffled out of the freezer like a backwards locomotive train, holding two frosty boxes.

'All right, Will, love?' she asked, while also grinning and chewing gum. 'Pizza okay, Jim Wimple?' She always calls me by my full name, and she knows I love pizza. 'Oven's on. It'll be ten minutes.'

Then she stopped still and shut her eyes. Had her chewing gum got lodged? Did she need the Heimlich manoeuvre? The music suddenly got superloud and she punched the air and started dancing again.

'Cor, I love that bit,' she called up at the ceiling. '*DJ got dat beat, got dat beat*,' she sang.

I could watch Will's mum dance for hours – it's all jerky and lively. But Fiona came in and turned the little radio off.

'I was enjoying that, love,' said Mrs Maggot, but not in an aggressive way.

'It's sad and pathetic,' Fiona stated in a way

that definitely was a bit aggressive. 'What you looking at?'

I realised that Fiona was talking to me – I had been staring at her. I do that.

I looked around me nervously. Will had disappeared. He does that.

'Well?' she demanded.

'I, er . . . I – er, wondered if you could tell me about your new scooter?' I fumbled. 'I saw it outside.'

'What do you want to know?' she asked casually, although I could see she was dying to talk about it. Her eyes sparkled like green glass under running water and she was having a hard time holding back the dimples that were forming at the corners of her mouth.

'It's a Bazoom!,' I said knowingly.

'Certainly is, my friend.' (I knew she'd said that as a kind of cool expression, but I locked it into my memory bank, *my friend*.) 'Just ten left when I got there and it was the last green one. Got it in the nick of time. Saved up for it myself too. What do you think?'

'It's amazing.'

'Well, of course it is. My friend is getting one, too and we're working on some busting moves. I'm going to try some out after tea,' she said. And then she talked lots and lots about these 'busting moves' and I gazed at her while I could get away with it. I'm not obsessed with Fiona or anything, but she's kind of fascinating . . . She's like half cat, half Viking. One minute she's cool and graceful and the next minute –

'But don't go thinking you and my squitty little brother can use it! Touch it and you're dead. Get it?'

After pizza – Hawaiian for me and Mediterranean Vegetable with a garnish of cornflakes for Will – we went up to Will's room. Will's brain is a bit messy, like spaghetti, but his room is stupidly neat and tidy. Every shelf has a label like in the library – History, General Reference, Fiction. But he has more than just books. There are shelves for Fossils, Items Found on Road, Lego Models (Permanent), Lego Models (Temporary Exhibition), Snail Shells, Snails (Alive) and Molluscs (Dead). He visits those last three shelves the most.

Will loves snails. His favourite bedtime book is *The Big Book of Molluscs*.

'Let's get Maximus out for measuring,' Will suggested. Without waiting for an answer he climbed the stepladder and brought down the tank containing a slow-growing baby giant African land snail. Maximus was hibernating, so Will placed him on the floor between us. He was about as interesting as a stone.

'You have got to be kidding me!' exclaimed Fiona, poking her head round the door. 'There's rock legends, there's astronauts on the moon and then there's you two, staring at a creature that's so bored it can't be bothered to move,' She muttered 'losers' as she shut the door, which wasn't very nice. She was still in Viking mood, then . . .

'There are no astronauts on the moon,' Will shouted after her. 'The next mission isn't for three months!'

'Whatever!' called Fiona from the bottom of the stairs.

'And it's not only rock legends, astronauts and us, is it?' Will asked me. 'There are quite a few other people populating the globe: clowns, roadsweepers . . .'

The front door slammed downstairs and I casually moved to Will's bedroom window as he continued his list. Below me, Fiona was mounting her beetle-green Bazoom!. She had tied her dark hair into twin ponytails. She moved the scooter out into the street and steadied her foot on the base. Then she pressed her pop-boost and sped down the road. I heard her whoop as it wobbled a bit, but she mastered it within seconds, turning easily and boost-scooting back up the road so smoothly . . . it was like she was born to ride a Bazoom!.

'. . . and there are palaeontologists who study creatures that don't move. And that is why, Jim Wimple, you should never take any notice of my sister.'

That was impossible, I thought, although I couldn't tell that to Will.

After determining that Maximus's minuscule

growth wasn't measurable with a school ruler, I headed home.

As I scooted on my boring, foot-powered, gadgetless, three-year-old scooter, I kept thinking about Fiona on her new Bazoom! – her excited green eyes, her dimples, the way she said 'my friend'. I turned the corner into my road (which has semi-detached houses and less friendly neighbours), and that's when it hit me: now that she had her beetle-green speeding machine, there was no way Fiona would be scooting to school with us. She'd be zooming. From now on Will and I would be on our own. I might never get to chat with Fiona properly again!

I felt a flutter of panic somewhere in my stomach, and in that instant the Bazoom! was no longer just a daydream along with flying suits with fully functioning detachable wings – the Bazoom! was *the answer to everything*.

Why? Because Bazoom!s were epic. If I got a Bazoom! I'd be cool. And if I got a Bazoom!, Will and I would be able to keep up with Fiona.

Better still, if I got a Bazoom! I could do pavement jumps and Fiona might say something like 'Cool tricks, Jim!' and ask to see more. She might even look at me normally – I mean, without the face of a disgruntled Viking queen.

The more I thought about it the more I realised that this was definitely something worth getting my guts in a twist over.

I had to get a Bazoom!.

Chapter 2

When I got home, Mum was using both hands to push spinach into her juicing machine, which was screeching like a tortured Dalek. She turned it off when she saw me and it slowed with a rattle and a wheeze.

'Hello, darling,' she called. 'Hungry? There's mushroom fritters in the fridge.'

'No thanks. I've eaten,' I said.

'What did they feed you?'

Once, I admitted to eating a hot dog and

crisps at Will's house and she made me eat Super-Seed Smoothies for ten days straight. If I never saw another Super-Seed Smoothie again it would be too soon, but I didn't want to lie. I decided to distract her, instead.

'What are you making there, Mum?'

'A juice creation! Want some?'

I shook my head. If you've met my mum before, you'll know why. If you haven't, then I'd better tell you a bit about her. Mum's a health nut. She owns an online health food shop called the The Happy Husk and creates her own healthy recipes. I swear they are so weird that Dr Who's sonic screwdriver would explode on analysis.

'Come on, Jim,' she pleaded sweetly. 'I've been adjusting the recipe all afternoon. I think I've cracked it!'

I looked at the dark green gunk.

'There's a truckload of antioxidants in every drop.' She widened her eyes and nodded, as if this was tempting information.

I was close to pulling a rude face. But at some point I had to ask the big Bazoom! question and I needed my parents to be in a very good mood when I did. Bazoom!s were serious business. Worth sacrificing your taste buds for.

I nodded and rubbed my tummy, instead. As she poured the mixture into two glasses it made ploppy belching sounds. It smelled of cowsheds.

'It'll do you the world of good,' Mum beamed. 'Here, I'll have one with you.'

She knocked hers back straight away, which was off-putting because some of it got stuck on her top lip and I could see what I was in for. *Down in one*, I thought to myself. *Get it over with*. I swigged it fast. It tasted like freshly ploughed fields – cowpats and all.

"S'licious, Mum,' I croaked.

'Wonderful! I'll put that down as a success, yes? What shall we call it . . . Spring Clean?'

'It's autumn,' I reminded her.

'Well, it has all the colours of spring,' she insisted.

I looked at the sludge. I thought it had all the colours of a neglected swamp, but some things aren't worth arguing about.

'What time is Dad home?'

'He'll be home a bit late tonight,' she said. 'But tell you what, if you help me finish this off, I'll let you stay up and wait for him.' She jiggled the jug of Spring Clean.

'Oh . . . Okay, great,' I grimaced.

If you're wondering why I didn't ask Mum for a Bazoom! there and then it's because, as you now know, Mum is very focused on being healthy. Part of being healthy is avoiding death, and a big part of avoiding death is preventing accidents. For the first two years of my life I wore a home-made romper suit made of bubble wrap. Seriously. It was hard enough getting her to buy me a regular scooter – if I asked her for a boostable Bazoom! she'd say NO WAY, DANGER, AMBULANCE, END OF STORY!

Dad's a much softer touch. And if I could get Dad to say yes to a Bazoom! then he'd back me up when I asked Mum, just like he did with other dangerous things I have in my life – like my normal scooter, my bike, and my bunk bed . . .

My sister skipped into the kitchen as I was finishing off the Spring Clean (and trying very hard not to bring it back up).

'Urrrr, what's that around your mouth?' She pointed a finger at my face.

Mum smiled. 'Hello, Hetty. Would you like some, too? It's called Spring Clean.'

'No. It looks like cow doo-doo,' Hetty sneered. Mum laughed, completely oblivious.

Hetty helped herself to a Ribena drink instead and Mum just let her, though she's normally really strict about sugary drinks. Sometimes she doesn't have the energy to argue with Hetty and I don't blame her. Arguing with Hetty takes stamina.

'Hetty, could you make one of those for me too?' I croaked.

'And undo all that goodness, Jim? I don't think so,' Mum interrupted.

Hetty slid me a sly grin and slipped out of the kitchen with a big glass of squash and a couple of two-pence coins that had been sitting on the table.

Somehow Hetty gets away with everything. She may look sweet and innocent but in actual fact she's naughty and rude. And she's *brilliant*. Get this: she once made my parents sign a contract promising to buy her a My Little Pony. Afterwards she demanded a real pony, saying she meant MY as in it belonging to her, and LITTLE as in it being a Shetland pony, which is a short-legged horse. Dad bought her riding lessons to shut her up. (I told you he was a soft touch.)

I was pretty sure he would say yes to my request for a Bazoom!, but I wasn't absolutely certain. If anyone knew how to close a deal it was Hetty. So I followed her upstairs and knocked on her door.

'Not today, thank you,' she called from inside.

'Hetty, it's me,' I said. 'I need your advice.'

'The advice desk is closed.'

'Heather . . .' I said in my low voice. Heather is Hetty's real name. We use it when we're cross. 'Heather, let me in. I know about your horse fund.'

'Desk is open now. Come in.'

Hetty's room is in total chaos. It's like burglars have upturned everything in a search for jewels and cash. Although she doesn't have jewels, Hetty does have quite a bit of cash: a growing pile of two-pence coins she 'finds' around the house. Or steals, more like. She's saving up for a horse – that's her 'horse fund'.

'Take a seat, please,' she said, pointing to the floor.

I couldn't see the floor for mess, so I sat on a comfy-looking pile of clothes.

'Hetty, there's something I want really badly.'

'A haircut? I can give you one.'

I looked at Hetty's wonky self-styled fringe. She insisted on cutting it herself because apparently her hair 'didn't like strangers'.

'Maybe another time, Hetty. I need to ask Dad for something. If you wanted something badly, what would you say to him?'

Hetty tapped her chin. She must have seen people doing that on TV.

'I would find out one of his secrets and threaten to tell everyone if he didn't buy me what I wanted.'

'That's blackmail, you know!'

'Of course I know. I invented it,' Hetty huffed. 'And anyway, Dad doesn't have secrets.'

'I bet he does,' Hetty said, waggling her eyebrows. 'Everybody does. Secrets make the world go round. Do you want to know one of mine?'

I nodded.

'I hit Wayne at school today.'

Hetty might look like a Twiglet, but I know my little sister can pack a punch. 'What for?'

'He was breathing too loudly.'

'You hit him? For *breathing*?'

She nodded matter-of-factly. 'Now you need to tell me one of your secrets.'

I shook my head.

'But you have to, that's how it works. Tell me or I'll cut your hair when you're asleep.'

'Don't you dare,' I said.

Hetty might have been comfortable with blackmail but it was definitely not my style. What a mean and heartless way to get what you wanted! There was no way I was going to be mean and heartless to Dad. Dad and I had a special bond. A trust. A father–son thing. Nothing was going to break that . . . No, there was another way – I'd just have to ask him. Very nicely.

That evening, while Mum did yoga in her 'garden studio' (which was a shed with a carpet), I tried to create a calm and relaxing atmosphere in the house ready for when Dad came home. Dad worked for an accountancy company called Mallet & Mullet and often worked late – probably because he always got stuck on some sums. He's not very good at maths, you see (I know, an accountant who's rubbish at maths – it's a bit embarrassing, really). It wasn't the ideal time to ask him for an expensive present, when he's late home and tired out from doing maths, but the Bazoom!s were running out. If Fiona had taken the tenth and her 'busting moves' friend was buying the ninth, there would only be eight left! Bazoom!s didn't wait for the perfect time to ask parents. So I plumped up the sofa cushions and popped in Dad's favourite DVD: *The Best Bits of Mr Bean*. And then I waited and waited and waited.

Later that evening Mum woke me up on the

sofa and told me that Dad had to work through the night and I needed to go to bed. Upstairs I found Hetty in my bed so I snuggled up next to her and she kicked me in the ribs all night long.

Chapter 3

The next morning I woke up with a pain in my chest, and it wasn't Hetty's foot. I'd dreamed that I was in a very long queue outside Scoots waiting to buy a Bazoom!, and people kept pushing in front of me so I got nowhere. Bazoom!s were running out fast and Fiona was shaking her head, as if to say 'too late' . . .

It was a sign that I needed to act fast. Where was Dad? I had to ask him immediately!

Hetty was snore-whistling in deep sleep, so I

carefully rolled out of bed and headed for my parents' room. I stopped on the landing, frozen by the magnitude of the task ahead . . .

Yes, I had to ask Dad right away – but I also had to ask *the right way*, because this wasn't like asking for a football or a skateboard. Bazoom!s were super expensive. I had to be very persuasive and I wasn't totally confident that my natural persuasiveness was persuasive enough. I needed back-up.

Although his brain is a bit like spaghetti, Will Maggot is also really clever, like Einstein. Will is Spagstein, and sometimes he'll come out with a meatball of brilliance. So, with my fingers crossed for a meatball, I called him from the upstairs phone at the end of the landing.

'I'm seeing you in twenty minutes,' he said. 'We go to school together.'

'I know, but I need your advice and it can't wait,' I whispered. 'I'm going to ask Dad for a Bazoom! and I need to be really, really persuasive. Do you have any ideas?'

I heard him put the phone down. I knew he'd be going to his bedroom to look for a book. Probably one on his Reference shelf. Just then, Hetty came onto the landing clutching Bo-Bo (an old teddy bear that looked more like roadkill).

'What you doing?' she murmured, cocking her head to the side.

'Nothing,' I whispered. 'Go back to bed.'

'I was hoping you'd saying something interesting in your sleep last night, but you didn't. So you still owe me a secret . . .' She yawned, stumbling towards her own bedroom, thankfully too bleary to question why I had a telephone receiver to my ear.

Then there was sudden heavy breathing.

'Use good *ethos*, *pathos* and *logos*,' Will told me, panting a little.

'What?'

'*Ethos* is character, *pathos* is feeling and *logos* is reasoning. Be good, be passionate and be sensible. And . . .'

'And?'

'And last night I had a dream about a giant squid, Jim, but I'll tell you later.'

The phone went dead. Forgetting the giant squid, I was left with ethos, pathos and logos. The first one – character – was okay, because I already had good character (I hardly ever got told off). If that's all it took, being me with extra me-ness – Jim Supreme – then I was one step closer.

The next step was pathos – passion. I just had to ask Dad for a Bazoom! with lots and lots of passion. Well, that wasn't going to be hard.

I found him the kitchen, looking nervous. I recognised that look. It meant Mum was making breakfast. She was crouched by a low cupboard and every two seconds her arm flew up with another ingredient to put on the kitchen counter.

'Flaxseed, oatbran, sunflower seeds . . . '

'Hi Mum, hi Dad.'

'Morning, Jim,' Dad said shakily. 'Your mum's just making me a breakfast drink.'

'So I can see . . .' I smiled at him pityingly.

'It's called the Get Up and Go!' Mum called from under the counter.

'I'm tempted to get up and go,' Dad said out of the corner of his mouth, nudging me.

'Right, then,' Mum said, standing upright. 'Let's get this breakfast on the road!'

'I'm tempted to get breakfast on the road,' Dad whispered, nudging me again. I giggled.

Mum tipped the contents of various packets – brown powders, ugly seeds, dried dandelions – into a jug with orange juice, then whizzed them all together with a blender to make grey sludge. Dad and I both held our hands to our mouths with disgust. It was too much, too much even for Jim Supreme. It was time for a 'scram sandwich'*.

'Mum, I'm in a real hurry. Can you save some for me?'

'Sure will,' she said with a happy smile.

'And Dad,' I said, putting my hand in his. 'Can I have a quiet word with you?'

'What is it, son?' he asked, bending over so we were eye to eye.

* (That's my favourite saying by the way – isn't it catchy?)

'Dad. You know I don't usually ask you for anything –' I started.

'Speaking of asking for things,' he interrupted in hushed tones, 'could you dispose of this on the way to school for me?' Dad handed me a foil wrapper containing rock-solid biscuits. 'Your mum's made mid-morning snacks for my work colleagues.' He winced. 'Last time, my secretary chipped her front tooth.'

'Okay,' I smiled, stuffing them in my rucksack. 'Can I ask *you* for something now?'

'Yes, son, of course, absolutely anything,' Dad said warmly. This is why I loved Dad – nothing was ever a problem. This was going to be easier than I thought.

'Please can I have a Bazoom!?'

'A what?'

'It's a scooter. It has a pop-boost and it's so awesome and it's –'

'What did you say it was called again?' he asked, concentrating. His eyebrows were bunched together.

'A Bazoom!!'

Dad closed his eyes as if he were thinking really hard. I waited for him to pop them open with a big smile and cry YES!, like he did when we played peek-a-boo when I was little – but he was frozen, eyes closed.

I turned up the pathos to help him think faster. 'Dad, I *really* want one. It's the only thing I've ever wanted. I'll be *so* happy. The happiest I've ever been. Dad? What do you say? Can I have a Bazoom!?'

Suddenly his eyes flew open like I knew they would. But he wasn't smiling.

'No,' he said quietly.

I was overwhelmed with disappointment. I was so sure Dad would say YES, what with

his no-problem personality. He had said NO
– just NO, without any explanation. Usually
he said things like 'No, because . . .' or 'Let's
talk about it again next week' or 'No, but when
your mum's gone I'll say yes, okay?'. A straight
NO wasn't like Dad at all. And what about
my ethos and pathos, and all the favours I did
him, like getting rid of Mum's biscuits? I
couldn't believe it! I didn't understand.

I looked up at him – he was standing tall and
stiff and his face was dark. Perhaps he was
stressed. Perhaps he was really behind with his
maths at work.

On Tuesdays, Streets the Newsagent has crisp
deliveries so the shop opens early, and Will and
Fiona and I pop in on the way to school. Will
always buys a Curly Wurly because he says it
reminds him of the complexity of life. Fiona

buys a tube of Brain-Sparks (popping candy chewy sweets) and I get crisps – fresh crisps, straight off the delivery truck. I love crisps. But today Fiona wasn't with us – she was going on her green dream machine, just as I feared – and, as Will and I went to school alone, my crisps didn't seem to taste as good as they usually did. And everywhere I looked I saw kids on cool scooters.

It made me feel uncool and boring. I think it's called envy, and I couldn't hold it in. The more I thought about not having a Bazoom! the more I absolutely had to have one. I told Will about my epic failure with Dad.

'. . . And I tried showing Ethos and Pathos,' I explained, throwing my hands in the air.

Will snorted. 'I don't think travel brochures of the Greek islands are going to help!' he said, and he rolled his eyes as if I was barking mad.

I wondered if I'd pronounced it wrong, but I didn't say anything. Some things aren't worth arguing about.

'I'm going to have to find another way,' I said, crunching a big crisp for effect.

'Can I tell you about my giant squid dream?'

'Later, Will. There are many important things in life and this is one of them,' I said.

'What are the others?' Will asked earnestly, scrunching his face like a flannel.

'Water, medicine, stuff like that . . . Look, that's not important –'

'But you just said they were important,' Will protested.

'They are but I'm gearing up to talk about the Bazoom!.'

'Bazoom!s don't have gears – they're scooters.' I sighed.

It looked as if it might be one of those days

when Will was more spaghetti than Einstein. Not even Spagstein, just Spag.

'I need a Bazoom!,' I said emphatically. Then, as an idea came to me, I said, 'We *both* do.'

Right now you probably don't believe that Will could produce a mental meatball of brilliance. But he can. It's just that they're hidden in the spaghetti – you need to look for them. I was ready to search through everything he said, so long as he said something quickly, before Fiona's dimples disappeared forever and Scoots ran out of Bazoom!s. I couldn't tell Will the bit about Fiona, but I needed to tell him something – something *mega* – so he would help me think up a plan . . . Scooter tricks and speed-boosts weren't the things Will's dreams were made of – snail-slow Will would not be motivated by Bazoom!s alone . . .

So I told Will that Jeremy Flowers was after us.

Shouting in the street is just a warm-up – Jeremy Flowers can be seriously horrible. He once reported his mum for robbery. She'd only taken his pants from his bedroom floor for washing, but uniformed police officers turned up with sirens and flashing lights. It was in the local paper. Jeremy Flowers was capable of anything, and Will was terrified of him.

'He said we were next on his list,' I told him.

'Next on his list for what?' said Will, his eyes wide like slices of boiled egg.

'He said we'd find out next time he caught up with us.' I crossed my fingers behind my back and hoped that lying for a good cause was forgiveable. 'If we don't have Fiona, we don't have protection,' I said. 'But if I get a Bazoom!

we can both ride it, and there's no way Jeremy could catch us. We'd be way too fast.'

There was a sudden *POP!* – like a car backfiring – and Fiona zoomed right between us. Her dark hair was coiled into buns either side of her head, and she had a cloth school bag slung over one shoulder that she'd scribbled on with felt-tip pens.

'Wait!' Will called, nearly crying.

'See you later, losers!'

She spat the words at us like a she-Viking gobbing into a fire pit, pressed the pop-boost and sped ahead even faster, turning and flashing her cruel green eyes.

'Oh flapjacks!' Will exclaimed as we watched her ride into the distance. 'We really need to get a Bazoom!.'

My crisps began to taste extra salt 'n' vinegary now that I had Will on board, and we scooted on, me feeling hopeful and Will feeling fearful. He kept watch for Jeremy Flowers as I told him about Dad.

'He said NO,' Will repeated. 'Nothing else?'

'That was the weird thing. He didn't explain, he just said NO.'

'Excellent. There's hope.'

'Will, there'd have been hope if he'd said maybe. But he said no.'

'NO has a flip side. All you have to do is flip it over to a YES.'

'And it's easy flipping a NO into a YES, is it?'

'Yes. Or no. Depending which way you look at it.'

I began to wonder if Will's spaghetti was overcooked.

'So how do we flip it to a YES?'

Will stopped scooting and I pulled up alongside.

'What is it?' I said.

He put his fingers either side of his head and waggled them against my face.

'What are you doing, Will?'

'Just feel what I'm telling you,' Will whispered and waggled them at me again.

'Are you a bull?'

'No!' he said crossly. 'Concentrate on what I'm transmitting . . .'

'Are you a donkey?'

Will shook his head.

I felt a wave of disappointment crash over me as I realised what it was.

'You're a snail, aren't you?'

Will always finds a way to talk about snails. It's as though his brain is so full of snail facts they simply leak out. If you point out an irrelevant snail fact that's slipped into conversation he says, 'The whole world is connected, Jim, the whole world is connected.'

'It's snail touch-telepathy,' Will explained, his fingers still on his head and still trying to prod my cheek.

'Snail telepathy?' I groaned. 'Please tell me you're joking.'

'The whole world is connected, Jim, and snails can connect by telepathy. All they have to do is touch each other. If you touch your dad while thinking about the Bazoom! . . .'

I pulled a face.

'It won't work if your heart's not in it,' Will whispered.

'It won't work if I'm not a snail,' I replied.

There was a thundering of feet.

As we turned, Jeremy Flowers ran into view, laughing maniacally and exposing his hookworm teeth. He was chasing some poor kid across the road. Will and I scrambled into a front garden and hid behind the wall.

'That was close,' Will panted. 'We have *got* to get that Bazoom!.'

I was glad he was taking it seriously. Our eyes were on the bully, just metres away. He had grabbed the kid's bag and was now stamping on it, shouting, 'Mash you up, mash you up', as the kid stood by and whimpered. Will held his bag close to his chest protectively and began to whimper too.

'Shh,' I hissed. 'He'll hear us.' But Will was starting to tremble, his bottom lip was quivering and I heard the first squeaks of a nervous scream forming in his throat.

Will's relationship with Jeremy Flowers isn't a good one. Once upon a time Will was trying to rescue a snail in the middle of the playground when Jeremy stamped on it – on purpose! (That's the stamp story I was going to tell you.) Will never got over it. But if he didn't control himself Jeremy was going to stamp on *us*! I took Will's face in my hands and turned it towards me.

'Now listen, you can't keep letting yourself think about that day.'

Will didn't respond. His face was still in my hands, heavy like a bag of potatoes, and his breathing was raspy.

'Will!' I said again, shaking his head a little. 'Will, breathe normally. We're safe . . . For now,' I added hurriedly. 'Think about the Bazoom! instead. We need that Bazoom!. How are we going to get one? Focus!'

He blinked slowly like he was imagining white fluffy clouds drifting across a summer sky.

'Think about that day,' he said gormlessly. 'Pop into your mind . . .'

'Will!'

'Pop into . . .'

'*Will!*' I urged. 'Snap out of it!'

'POP! Yes! That's it,' he said. 'Well done, Jim.'

'Well done for what?'

'For giving me an idea.'

'Is this anything to do with snails?'

Will promised his next idea was not snaily. He said hidden messages – or subliminal messaging, as it was called – was a real thing done by real people to sneak ideas into our minds. It was probably the reason I liked burgers so much, he said.

'Most kids like burgers,' I argued.

'But maybe most kids like burgers because there are burger messages hiding in television programmes.'

'Or maybe burgers are just yummy,' I shrugged.

'What about the gherkin slice?' Will protested. 'I mean, have you *seen* a gherkin? Who would choose to like a gherkin? In Connecticut, America, a gherkin isn't officially a gherkin unless you can bounce it off the floor. But people in Connecticut still eat burgers. You have to ask yourself why.'

That was a perfect and puzzling example of the internal workings of Will Maggot's brain. But maybe he was right. Maybe subliminal messaging was everywhere. Because Will was into *Spongebob Squarepants* in a big way and said it was 'the best show about the bottom of the sea on the face of the earth'. You have to ask yourself why.

That afternoon Will's mum was having some friends over to drink fizzy wine and look at jewellery brochures, so Will came over to my house to discuss Operation Bazoom!. He stood on the top bunk and rearranged the glow stars on my ceiling. I did some computer research about subliminal messaging. It didn't look promising.

'Subliminal messaging doesn't seem to have a high success rate . . .' I said.

'I think Milky Way constellations are boring – they're all mammals,' Will mused.

'But what do you think about what I just said, about subliminal messaging, Will?'

'They look more like plankton, really,' he mumbled to himself.

'Okay, subliminal messaging is out,' I decided. 'But I do like the idea of finding a way of getting Dad to say yes to a Bazoom! without really thinking about it. We need to get his attention without getting *too much* of his attention.'

Will climbed down from the desk. He looked up at his new constellation and rubbed his neck.

'If you want to make rude faces at a koala, do it while it's eating gum leaves,' he said.

'And what about Dad?' I asked, shaking my head, confused.

'Your dad doesn't eat gum leaves.'

'No, he doesn't,' I said, gritting my teeth slightly, 'because my dad isn't a koala.'

'No. He's an accountant, isn't he?' Will said, climbing back onto the bunk to adjust a star. 'So I'd make rude faces at him when he was at work. Accountants concentrate at work. Especially your dad – he's rubbish at maths.' Will looked down and smiled.

Bingo, the meatball!

Chapter 4

On Wednesday, Will and I sat under the tree at the back of the playing fields during break (well away from Jeremy Flowers) and worked out the finer details of Operation Bazoom!.

We agreed that anything too close to subliminal messaging was out – even if it *did* work, there was no guarantee we would brainwash the right person. What if Dad's secretary kept seeing the messages and became obsessed by Bazoom!s? What if she went and bought the last one? What if she bought the last one, fell off it and chipped another tooth? It was risky in so many ways.

But Will's meatball had rolled. And it was disguised as a gum-chewing koala bear hard at work. *Work* was the operative word. The final plan was this: we would go to Dad's workplace and leave a message somewhere everyone could see it but that was only addressed to Dad. We named it the 'Letter of Persuasion' and it read like this:

Dear Daddy,
I hope you're having a lovely day at work
with your really nice work colleagues.
Please can I get a Bazoom!? I'll be good
and tidy my room (and Hetty's room). It
will make me so happy.
Love,
Jim.

It was a winner, because:

1. Dad would be occupied with difficult maths and by comparison saying yes to a Bazoom! would be easy, and
2. He'd want to look like a generous father in front of all his colleagues, who would already be going 'aw, sweet . . .' at the bit that says, *I hope you're having a lovely day at work with your really nice work colleagues.*

Will and I high-fived. It was Bazoom!-gettingly brilliant.

And that's how the plan to visit Dad's office came about, and how we then found ourselves answering Dad's telephone, talking about blood and freaking out just a little bit.

That evening I left Mum and Dad on the sofa watching *Mr Bean* and said I was going to Will's house to do homework. Hetty, who'd been watching me like a hawk, wanted to come but I said she couldn't. I said Will and I would be concocting a plan to get rid of Jeremy Flowers, the school bully, and we might say words six-year-olds shouldn't hear.

'I know bad words, and I know Jeremy Flowers,' she protested.

'I don't think you do,' I laughed. 'And for the last time, the answer is no.'

'Did you get what you wanted from Dad yet?' she asked.

'Not yet.'

'Two words, little brother: black and mail,' she winked.

'I'm not your little brother,' I objected. 'And I will never, *ever* use blackmail.'

But as I set off, I wasn't sure if I believed that. If our plan didn't go to plan, it might be the only choice I had. As a last resort, though. An absolute last resort. I just needed to have a secret up my sleeve. It wouldn't hurt to be prepared.

Will and I weren't meeting at his house. We were going into town to place the Letter of Persuasion at Dad's work. He was waiting for me, as arranged, outside Scoots.

'You're dressed in dark blue,' I noted.

Will was head to toe in blue trainers, tight blue leggings (I hoped they were Fiona's) and a tight blue top with the hood up. He did a little twirl to show me the full effect.

'Great, but *why* are you dressed in dark blue?' I asked.

'It's camouflage,' he said under his breath, secretively. 'Against the night sky . . .'

'I see,' I said. 'But we're going inside a building. And it's light.'

'Well, I'm more camouflaged than you!' He pointed at my clothes – jeans and a bright green T-shirt saying *Give Chickpeas A Chance*. It had been a birthday present from Mum. It was all I could find in the clean-clothes pile. 'If things go wrong you'll regret that choice.'

Will was right – in Will's world. But in the real world nothing was going to go wrong, because the plan was simple. It was to be carried out in three phases.

1. Go into Dad's office
2. Plant the Letter of Persuasion
3. Leave the office

There was also another in-between phase that I had just invented. I didn't tell Will about it in case it got too complicated. And also because I didn't want him to think I was sneaky and heartless.

Phase 2.5 was Gathering Secrets for Blackmail or, as I preferred to think of it, Hettymail. It required getting my hands on something I shouldn't – something a dad wouldn't want his son to see, let alone the rest of the world, like a telling off from his boss about his bad maths. Or proof he'd been eating from a hamburger restaurant with an unhealthy reputation. But it was just in case of emergencies. A last resort. A back-up. A plan B. You understand, it's not normally my style . . .

As Will synchronised the watch on his left hand with the watch on his right hand, I peered in through the Scoots shop window. There was a big Bazoom! display. A to-die-for scooter (a red one!) was positioned in the middle of the

window surrounded by cardboard cut-out
people wearing sunglasses and T-shirts saying
'Wowsers', 'Check it out!' and 'Boost-tastic!'
Hanging from the ceiling above was a big digital

counter which said '8 LEFT'. Time was running out.

'Come on, Will. It's time for a scram sandwich!' My special expression didn't seem to work. Will was still adjusting the numbers and beeps on his wrist. 'Come on, Will, we don't need watches.'

'Don't we?' he asked in a deeply mysterious tone.

'I've got the Letter of Persuasion ready,' I informed him.

'But have you got what it takes?' he asked me in return, waggling his eyebrows.

'Er, yes.'

'Then let's do it!' he said, patting my back.

Will wasn't being very Will-ish. He was being kind of 'macho'.

'Will, have you been watching any action movies recently?'

'Sure have,' he replied, grinning. 'Watched one just before I came out.'

'Any particular reason?'

'Mission survival.'

'Explain.'

'I saw a nature programme about how chameleons change colour when they're in danger. So to see how humans survive danger you have to watch action movies because people are always in danger in action movies. But you need to focus on the characters that don't die.'

'Okay. What did you learn?'

'If you flatten your body against a wall you become invisible, and a wristwatch is useful. Stands to reason two watches are doubly useful.'

'I see . . .' I said. 'Which action movie did you watch?'

'One about a boy who discovers a shipment

of guns on a cruise liner and makes friends with a maverick detective.'

Will's enthusiasm was great, but I hoped he wasn't planning to recreate any action movie scenes. Operation Bazoom! was a simple in/out exercise. We didn't need to complicate it with stealth moves or drop 'n' roll manoeuvres across the floor.

From there we scooted to Dad's office building in total silence, our minds fixed on what we had to do and why we had to do it. Well, my mind was fixed on that. Will could have been thinking about the terminal velocity of a catapulted peanut. You could never tell.

Dad's office building was very modern, with the words Mallet & Mullet in large mirrored letters across the front. It had tall glass doors that opened automatically. Inside the foyer there were big flower displays and on the walls were large photographs of landmarks like the Taj Mahal and the Golden Gate Bridge. It looked so clean and posh I worried my trainers would leave dirty marks on the gleaming marble floor. We looked around the foyer. It was like a sealed cube. There was no way that we could see into the offices beyond or even how to get to them.

'Let's case the joint!' Will did a drop 'n' roll across the floor to the opposite side of the room and looked about. He shook his head. 'There must be a hidden door,' he whispered. He spun around and pressed his tummy flat against the wall, arms spread, shuffling like a crab, feeling for an edge or a crack. He kept knocking his head on the picture frames. He hit Mount Fuji particularly hard and it swung diagonally.

'Ow!' Will cupped his forehead and stamped

his foot, the way you do when you don't want to cry.

The wall to the right of the picture began to slide apart.

'It's open!' I said.

'Oh no . . . Now I'll need stitches,' Will moaned.

'Not your head, Will. The door!'

Will looked up, his eyes watery with pain. The wall sections that had slid apart stayed open long enough to see that there was a corridor beyond, and then they closed again. The picture was a trigger!

'Will, bang your head on Mount Fuji again, will you?'

Chapter 5

Beyond the door we were no longer surrounded by shiny modern decor. There were no marble floors and bright travel photographs. Instead we were walking down moth-eaten carpeted corridors which were peeling with old paint and smelled of musty books. On the walls were framed portraits – oil paintings and sketches. They were people who worked at Mallet & Mullet, we guessed. And there was one of Dad. He looked very serious – his face was long, his lips were thin and his low-down eyebrows looked as if they meant business. At home Dad was very smiley and his eyebrows danced at the top of his head, so in my opinion this was a really bad likeness by a really rubbish artist. But every single Mallet & Mullet portrait looked stern, although that's about all they had in common. Some wore old-fashioned hats and frilly collars, others had long hair or missing teeth or bony heads . . .

'What's all that about?' I whispered to Will, pointing to a man with a twizzly beard.

'Probably a joke. Accountants are famous for being funny.'

We passed a chalky sketch of a big-jawed man with eyebrows like weasels.

Will guffawed. 'A caveman could have done better than that!'

Everything was so *old*. Floorboards creaked

below the carpet and the pictures on the walls were covered in dust – my nose twitched with a sneeze as we passed them. The large wooden doors lining the corridors were dull and ancient, sticky with layers of polish and varnish. They had big round brass handles and nameplates with fancy writing that was hard to read.

We heard a small cough and the padding of feet coming from further down the corridor. I copied Will and flattened myself against the wall, hoping it would make us invisible. The woman walking towards us was looking down at the papers she was holding. Just feet away she stopped and yawned and, just before she blocked her yawn with a hand, I spotted it – a chipped front tooth. It was Dad's secretary! She went into an office on our left with a nameplate that said G. *Reaper* . . .

G. Reaper?

A few moments later she stepped out into the
corridor again and headed back the way she
came. We decided to check out the office. It
didn't have Dad's name on it, but the place was
so old the nameplate could have been there for
centuries . . . Will looked at his watches several

times. Then he made some hand signals: one fist with two fingers up, then two fists and a downwards thumb. I wasn't entirely sure what they meant – it looked more like animal shadow puppets – but it was probably something to do with the action movie. We opened the door. It was Dad's office all right. On the desk was a framed photo I recognised of me buried in beach sand and Hetty standing with her foot on my head like a trophy hunter.

'You know what to do!' Will whispered, action-hero style. Then he did a hand signal (an emu?) and we moved inside. Will was in charge of keeping watch in the doorway while I placed the Letter of Persuasion (and snooped for secrets).

'Will!' I called. He edged away from the door towards me, flicking his head side to side as an efficient lookout should. 'What's the point of leaving the note if no one apart from Dad will see it? It doesn't look as if anyone else works in this office . . . Actually, it doesn't even look as if *Dad* works here. There's no computer! How weird is that?!'

Will ran round the room, dropped to the floor and searched under the desk. He rolled back out again, got to his feet and shook his head. We looked at each other like lemons, then took a good look around us. The office had a threadbare gold-coloured carpet and contained a desk, a big lamp, two bookshelves and an antique wardrobe that held a row of black cloaks and two pairs of nifty white trainers (which can't have been Dad's because he doesn't go to the gym or jog). That was it. Dad's desk was just a desk with nothing on it apart from the photo of me and Hetty and a weird little machine made of wood and metal. Maybe he'd tidied everything away . . . Rat's bums! This wasn't going to plan. How was the Letter of Persuasion going to have any impact in an empty room – and how was I going to find what I needed for Hettymail?

'Look at this . . .' said Will. He was standing by the bookcase and on the wall next to it was a felt board. At the top a sign was fixed with drawing pins. It said 'Trouble Clients', and underneath were photographs of old men and old ladies, all with deep wrinkles and fierce twinkly eyes.

'I know her!' Will said, pointing to a lady with a set of marvellous white teeth and hair dyed orang-utan orange. 'That's Audrey Finnigan. She owns three parrots, lives in our street. I never knew she was troublesome, Jim. Do you think your dad'll punish her?'

'Dad doesn't know the meaning of

punishment,' I said. 'Unless you count being made to watch his *Great Trains of Our Time* DVD!'

Trainspotting was Dad's hobby. He did it for relaxation. Obviously when you have 'Trouble Clients' relaxation is very important.

Deafeningly loud, the metal machine made a sudden ringing sound and rattled with the effort. Turns out it was an ancient telephone. Will knew all about old phones from his twentieth-century telecommunications catalogue and showed me how it worked. He pointed out the number dial and the voice piece, then lifted the handset . . . And accidentally answered the call.

Before we could say anything, a gravelly voice began speaking on the other end. It was Dad's boss.

'. . . *You haven't done blood before, I know that. But you can do it, and I have no doubt you're the best man for the job. I'm offering you a promotion. A pay rise. Will you think about it?'*

And that's when everything began to feel really weird.

Being in Dad's office suddenly didn't seem like such a good idea. It didn't feel right. There was no reason to be spooked; the lights were on and there were no creaking walls or ghostly wails, no pictures with moving eyes. But goosebumps had started to crawl up my arms.

'Ever get the feeling you're not supposed to be somewhere?' I whispered.

As soon as I said those words, I saw the hairs stand up on Will's arms too, and both of us got so spooked out we forgot what action film characters would do, and ran. We sprinted back along the corridor to the door at the end. It was sealed shut and our hearts were pounding. Will threw his arms in the air in despair. They fell clumsily, hitting the final portrait on the wall – a man with hollow cheeks – knocking it sideways. The doors opened and we fell through them and out into the foyer.

I realised that in the heat of the moment – the moment of feeling totally spooked – we'd forgotten all about the Letter of Persuasion.

Phase 1 and Phase 3 were a doddle, but we had left Mallet & Mullet without having completed phase 2. The mission had failed. Or had it? There was still Phase 2.5 . . .

Although I hadn't found out any of Dad's secrets, I had a feeling I'd stumbled on something – I didn't know what it was or what it meant – but it was definitely *something*, and something told me it was something I wasn't supposed to know. Phase 2.5 wasn't a success – but it wasn't dead in the water yet.

When I got home Mum was still sat in front of the television. She was eating her homemade lemon and horseradish cakes and pulling sour and spicy faces, one after the other.

'H-ah, J-hi-m,' she panted through the heat of a horseradish kick. 'Nice time at Will's?'

'Yeah . . . Where's Dad?' I asked. She swallowed hard and cleared her throat.

'Oh, he was here a while ago, but he had to go to work. Come and watch *The Great Cake Bake* with me. See what they did with that chocolate fudge cake there? I'm going to try that out, but swap the chocolate for maca powder. It's from the radish family, you know . . .'

Mum tried to explain how radishes were the new superfood, but my mind was somewhere else. It wasn't on Will. It wasn't on Fiona. It wasn't even on a Bazoom!. It was on Dad and how he was supposed to be at work. But he wasn't.

There was something fishy going on, and it wasn't Mum's cup of steaming anchovy tea.

Chapter 6

Upstairs I sat at my desk and got out a new project book.

I start projects whenever I have a burning question I need to work through, which is quite a lot. My shelves are full of project books with titles like *What Would I Do in a Parallel Life?*, *My Roof: Landing Pad for Alien Spaceships?*, *How Would I Survive an Alien Invasion?* and *How Can I Make Health Food Taste Nice?*

Despite the titles, most of my project books

end up covered in doodles and unfinished because I tend to get sidetracked by other thoughts like 'How Can I Earn More Pocket Money?' and 'What Makes Fiona Awesome?' (Please don't tell anyone that bit.) But this project would be different. I wouldn't get sidetracked. Because *this* project had two purposes:

a) working out how to flip Dad's NO to a YES, and

b) discovering the reasons behind his strange behaviour.

Everyone has secrets, Hetty had said.

My sister was a six-year-old pony enthusiast with a wonky fringe – hardly the brains of Scotland Yard – but I wondered if she had a point. After all, if I didn't know what Dad was thinking, *that* was a secret right there. And if I didn't know what he was doing, he might be doing something quite unexpected. Dad had become a big unknown. He had become a 'burning question' – one that deserved its own project book. The trouble was that *I* didn't know what I didn't know about Dad, so I had to start with all the stuff I *did* know and hope I could fill in the gaps.

I spread the project book on my desk and wrote:

Things I know about Dad

1. He can't do maths
2. He is an accountant
3. He loves *Mr Bean*
4. His hobby is trainspotting
5. He's hiding something

My heart skipped a beat when I wrote number five. I felt guilty even thinking about it. But there were a few things that made me uncertain – like the way he reacted when I asked for a Bazoom!, and the fact that Mum said he'd gone to work and, well, maybe he had, but I didn't see him. But I did see his office . . . and there weren't piles of papers, calculators and computers. I didn't see any pictures on the wall of old steam trains or Mr Bean. There wasn't even a vending machine for coffees and KitKats. It was soulless and creepy.

I wrote down some more points.

5. He works at Mallet & Mullet
6. His office is OLD, his telephone is OLD, he has problems with some OLD people
7. His office door doesn't say T. WIMPLE. It says G. REAPER
8. There are no computers

Most office workers have nine a.m. to five p.m. jobs. They work on computers, let their kids pop in to see them and talk about their day when they get home. But my dad worked all times of the day and night and I had never been invited to look round his office. He never talked about work, he never mentioned his colleagues (apart from Susan, the secretary with the chipped front tooth) and I don't think he's ever been to an office Christmas party. Mallet & Mullet seemed like a miserable, old-fashioned accountancy firm. Will said accountants were funny . . . Well, it didn't look like it. Either that, or Mallet & Mullet wasn't an accountancy firm . . .

Fear trickled down my spine.

I shook it off quickly. You can't jump to conclusions in an investigation – not without evidence. Before I let myself jump to any conclusions I needed more details. Had Will seen anything odd that I'd not noticed? I called him.

'Now you mention it, I was puzzled by the pictures in the foyer,' he said. 'Mount Fuji in particular. It didn't go with the Taj Mahal and the Eiffel Tower and the Golden Gate Bridge, you know? Mount Fuji is a natural wonder and the others are man-made.'

'Okay, did you see anything else strange?' I asked, writing 'Mount Fuji' in my project book.

'Nope. But I wasn't in detective mode. I was in action mode. My brain works in a totally different way in action mode.'

Will's brain worked in a totally different way to most people's whichever mode he was in, but I didn't say that.

'Red alert!' he shouted suddenly.

'What?'

'Just remembered. We need to flip the NO to a YES as soon as possible. Fiona told me her friend is getting a Bazoom! tomorrow. A yellow one. And then there'll only be seven Bazoom!s left. And if there are seven left, you may as well say there are six.'

'Why's that?'

'Because seven is everybody's favourite number – seven wonders of the world, seven colours in the rainbow, seven days in the week. A lot of people will see seven on the counter and be very tempted to buy a Bazoom!.'

'Okay, so let's say there are six,' I pondered. 'How long does that give us to do the flipping, do you think?'

'Depends how many people like the number six. Quite a few. It's everyone's favourite roll of the dice, isn't it? Oh, and then you've got five to worry about and, I'm telling you, five's a biggie. Four has its fans. Get down to three and we're really stuffed. Two –'

'Thanks, Will. I get the picture.'

And I did, I really did. Here I was listening to Will's number theories and trying to remember details about Dad's work when I could be killing two birds with one stone: I could be back at Mallet & Mullet flipping the NO into a YES with my Letter of Persuasion and at the same time getting to the bottom of Dad's mysterious job.

His office had given me a strong feeling that I wasn't supposed to be there. But I had to be brave.

I popped my project book, a torch and a pencil in my rucksack and crept out of my room. Hetty – who has senses like a bat, except when she's snoring – opened her bedroom door.

'What are you doing?' she asked me.

'Just going downstairs. It's gone eight o'clock – you should be in bed.'

'I've lost Bo-Bo.'

'Go to sleep, Hetty, and I promise Bo-Bo will be there in the morning.'

She narrowed her eyes suspiciously and very slowly shut the door. When I was sure she'd gone back to bed I tiptoed downstairs. I looked in at Mum, who was glued to her bakery programme, and quietly wheeled my bike – selected for speed – outside. My heart was pounding.

I looked left and right, up and down the street. There was a chill in the air, but I wasn't cold. I was fired up. I was in action mode.

Chapter 7

I had no plan. I'd done no preparation. I just turned up at Mallet & Mullet with the Letter of Persuasion in my backpack and a determination to discover the truth about Dad's work, and where he was. When the coast was clear I sneaked into the foyer and flattened myself against a wall behind an enormous potted fern. Then I scuttled to the other side of the room and nudged the picture on the wall. Nothing happened! I swung it violently on its hook, but still nothing happened. Rat's bums! Then I stood back and looked at the picture. It was the Taj Mahal. I saw Mount Fuji on the other side of the room and Will was right, it did look out of place, but not in the way he thought. It had been moved!

Could this be a security measure? It was clever, but why were Mallet & Mullet being so secretive? I ran over and tipped Mount Fuji and the wall next to it slid open.

This led into a different corridor to the one before, and I didn't know where I was. I couldn't see the office of G. Reaper, but there were plenty of other doors. They weren't all named. Some were downright random – like *The Glove Room* and *Brain Training*. Those goosebumps prickled once more. Nothing was going to persuade me to open those doors! . . . Eventually the corridor led to a door marked

General Office. If I was going to find out anything, I supposed, it was going to be here . . . I put my ear against the door – there was low murmuring and clicking. People at computers, perhaps! I opened the door a fraction and peered in . . .

There were lots of people in the General Office – LOTS. Some were sitting at desks flicking through large leather-bound registers, poring over maps, occasionally looking up to check a wall-mounted model of Great Britain, which was studded with miniature light bulbs that flashed red and green. I couldn't spot any keyboards – the clickety-clacking sound I'd heard was coming from a huge metal box twice as tall as me and at least five times wider. On one side of it people were punching little buttons and pulling levers, which made it whirr and rattle. On the other side of it, rickety numbers signs flipped over on a display board, like symbols on a fruit machine, and a team of workers furiously scribbled down the results with quill and ink. In the corner two employees looked as if they were getting ready to go jogging (pulling on nifty trainers like the ones I'd seen in Dad's office). They were all wearing cloaks – every single one of them – long, dark cloaks. Was it a Dress-Like-Dracula-for-Charity day? I searched the sea of cloaked people but I couldn't see Dad anywhere. Someone would be able to give me directions to his office, though. It was time to speak up. I opened the door wide and stepped through.

'Ahem.'

Everyone stopped what they were doing and looked up. There was total silence for a split second. Then they hid their scrolls and maps under their desks and started shouting numbers at each other. Odd, random lists and phrases like

'Twenty-five, sixty-nine, three hundred and forty-two', 'That'll be lots of tax' and 'Do the accounts right away!' Some smiled and nodded at me as they shouted. Others looked nervous.

One of the men who had been writing with a quill whipped off his black cloak (he had a normal suit and tie on underneath!) and moved towards me, cracking his knuckles. He stood very close with his hands on his hips and puffed out his chest, almost as if he was trying to block my view of the office.

'Hello, boy,' he said, smiling nervously. 'How did you get in here?'

'Er, the door was left open,' I replied. I didn't want them to know I'd figured out Mount Fuji. 'I'm looking for Terry Wimple's office,' I explained, trying to peek at the people behind him. The man shuffled sideways to block my view.

'Terry Wimple . . .' The man nodded and scratched his head. 'I don't think we have a Terry Wimple.'

'But . . . but . . . you must have,' I stuttered.

'Er, yes, we do have a Terry Wimple,' called a little voice from the back of the room. 'You know Terry. The really *natural* guy.'

The man in front of me looked up and grinned. 'Ah yes. Terry. Good old Terry.' He stopped smiling. 'Um, he's not here.'

'But I was told that he was at work,' I protested.

'Yes, yes. He was here,' the man flustered. 'But now, um . . .'

'He's gone to see a client,' said the helpful voice at the back of the room.

'Yes. He's gone out.'

'Okay,' I said. 'Sorry to disturb you.'

'Not at all,' said the man. 'Are you his son?'

I panicked. Should I tell the truth? I thought probably not.

'No. I'm no one,' I blurted. 'I'm nobody.'

'I see,' the man laughed. 'I'll show you out, Mr Nobody.'

I dodged to the side to get a look at the room behind him. 'Bye!' I called. They all started shouting numbers again. One woman did her best to hide the strange whirring clicking flipping machine by standing in front of it with her arms and legs stretched out like a starfish.

As soon as the door shut everything fell silent again and I heard someone say, 'How on earth did a kid get in here?'

Weirder than weird.

The man escorted me out of the building. I said goodbye in a cheery voice, but my body was shaking like a leaf. I leaned against my bike and closed my eyes.

'What are you doing?' hissed a voice just as a finger prodded my stomach. I nearly jumped out of my skin.

'Hetty!' She was standing right by my side, one hand on the handlebars of her pink sparkly unicorn bike.

'What are you doing?' she repeated.

'What am *I* doing? What are *you* doing?' I spat.

'*I* am keeping an eye on you, that's what I'm doing. Now you have to tell me what *you're* doing. That's how it works.'

'Does Mum know you're here? She'll go mad –'

'Don't be silly, of course she doesn't know.'

'Come on, we'd better get home before she finds out.'

'Tell me first,' she said, shaking her head and planting her feet solidly.

I realised that I was going to have to tell Hetty something. If I didn't she wouldn't move and then Mum's programme would finish and she'd discover both her children were missing. It would send her heart rhythms haywire.

'Okay. So I'm trying to find out a secret about Dad.'

'Really?' Hetty grinned wickedly. 'You took my advice, then. Where is he?'

'I don't know. He's not here. Listen, Hetty. Don't tell Mum or Dad I was here, okay?'

'That sounds like a secret to me. So you want me to keep *your* secret?' she said mischievously.

'Yes please.'

'You need to tell me another secret, then. That's how it works.'

I needed to get us both home before Mum sent

out a search party. But Hetty wasn't in a rush. She leaned her bike against the wall and crossed her arms across her chest – there was no way she'd be fobbed off with a silly pretend secret. It had to be good. It had to be something juicy.

'Okay. You know Fiona, Will's sister? Well, I have a kind of . . . thing. A crush. But you mustn't tell Will!' Hetty's eyes gleamed. 'Promise me, Hetty.'

Hetty winked and began cycling in the direction of home. I followed quickly.

We got back just in time to hear Mum's bakery programme ending. We kicked off our shoes, ran upstairs, jumped into bed and pretended to be asleep. But I couldn't sleep. Weird images were dancing in my head – of black cloaks and nifty trainers and people up to something they didn't want me to see.

Later that night I scribbled my observations in my project book:

1. Shifty behaviour
2. Nifty trainers
3. Shouting numbers – random?
4. Registers with names
5. Big machine – an ancient computer?
6. Terry Wimple. The natural guy

When I heard Dad come in later I crept downstairs rubbing my eyes, although I hadn't been asleep.

'Hi, Dad,' I mumbled, pretending to be sleepy.

'Oh, Jim!' he said. 'You startled me. Did I wake you up?'

I nodded. 'Why are you home so late?'

'Er, had to help some chap in Australia get his accounts sorted. Southern hemisphere time zones are such a nuisance. Did you know that it's now only four o'clock in the afternoon there? While you're snoozing they're getting ready to leave work and get home for a swim in the pool. Fancy that!'

I smiled and nodded and followed him into the kitchen. Dad was searching in the back of the cupboard for his secret stash of chocolate biscuits. When he found them he crammed one into his mouth and looked at me. He looked uneasy.

'Why don't you go to bed, Jim? It's late.'

'But I'm awake now,' I said.

'If I give you a biscuit and tell you a joke, will you go to bed afterwards?'

I nodded, taking a chocolate digestive.

'Okay. What's the difference between a coffin and a beginner's violin?'

I shook my head.

'The coffin has the dead person on the *in*side!' He slapped his thigh. 'Get it, Jim? Usually violin beginners make such awful sounds that people want to kill them . . . So the dead person's on the outside. See?'

'Oh right,' I said. It was hardly one of his best.

'Ah, well, I thought it was funny.'

'Dad,' I said carefully, 'What do you do at work?'

Dad gripped the edge of the kitchen table for a second, then paused to finish his mouthful of biscuit. 'Well, I make sure that companies have added up all the money they've made correctly, and then I subtract all the money they've spent. What's left over is called "profit". Then I tell them how much of their profit to pay the government in taxes.'

'That's a lot of maths, Dad!' I exclaimed,

before adding a playful giggle. 'How do you do it all?'

'Well, luckily we have lots of shiny high-tech, top of the range computers that do the maths for us,' Dad said. 'Is that cheating?'

'A little bit,' I said stiffly.

High-tech computers?!! He was lying. *Dad was lying!*

'You won't tell anyone, will you?' Dad nudged, grinning.

'No, I'll pretend you never told me,' I said with a weak smile and a bite of my biscuit. It didn't taste as good as it should, considering it was real chocolate and not made of radishes.

Dad laughed at that and gave me a really tight hug. It was so tight I could feel his heart thumping through his jumper and through my pyjamas. I breathed in his warmth. He usually gives me long hugs, the sort of hugs you need to escape from because you think you'll be starved of oxygen. But this was a short hug. He pulled away quickly.

'It is far too late for you to be awake,' he said sharply, and I noticed he was looking off colour like you do when you're ill or worried. 'Your mum will never forgive me if I don't send you to bed.'

'Okay. Goodnight, Dad,' I said.

''Night, Jim.' He ruffled the hair on my head and kissed the top of it.

At the doorway I turned to look at him one more time, and that's when I noticed he was wearing nifty trainers.

Chapter 8

Early the next morning I crept into Hetty's bedroom, found Bo-Bo (hanging from the ceiling light, where she must have thrown him) and tucked him into bed alongside her. I also left three two-pence coins on her bedside table for her horse fund. I hoped she'd keep my secret about Fiona – if she didn't, my friendship with Will might be in jeopardy and I dreaded to think how Fiona herself might react. She did kung fu for a start. She also did big-time humiliation, public and painful – Viking-style. Just thinking about it gave me the shivers.

So did the idea of seeing Dad. How would I be able to act normal after everything I saw last night? I'd stammer, blush, or say something stupid that would give me away . . . So I quickly got dressed, grabbed my project book and left a note in the kitchen saying I'd gone to Will's for breakfast.

'Hello Jim Wimple,' said Will's mum through a wedge of toast. 'Want some breakfast? Toast?'

Without waiting for my answer she let me in and I went through to the kitchen where Will was timing how long it took for his new cereal to go soggy in semi-skimmed milk. Last week it was Barley Malt Bombs with added iron (one minute, twenty seconds to sog). Today it was Choco-Asteroids, and they were hanging in there, still floating. Fiona was drinking a strawberry milkshake. She looked over her straw at me with her green cat-eyes and slurped it extra loudly, like a cat's warning hiss. I tried to wave in a friendly way but I think it came out a bit like a seal flapping its flipper. Why can't I ever act normal around Fiona?

'Two minutes, forty-eight seconds,' said Will as the first Asteroid sank. He looked up. 'All right, Jim?'

Mrs Maggot came in with her portable radio and started dancing in front of the toaster. Her bangles jangled with a tinny sound and Fiona's eyes rolled to the ceiling. She covered her ears with her hands and slurped even louder.

'Will, we need to talk,' I said. 'It's urgent.'

Will put his lips to the cereal bowl and drank the lot down.

'Disgusting,' Fiona muttered.

'It's efficient,' Will said. 'And breakfast should be the most efficient meal of the day.'

'Whatever,' Fiona said with no emotion whatsoever. Today was a Viking day, clearly.

'We're going to school, Mum,' Will shouted over the music.

'Hang on, Jim Wimple's toast will be ready in a minute,' she said, flashing me a smile. Her hips were still wiggling.

Will's dad walked in just as the toast popped and he grabbed it for himself.

'Oi, that was for our guest,' Will's mum said, slapping him playfully.

Will's dad didn't say much. In fact, I don't think I've ever heard him properly say anything. He just skulks around and grunts. He kissed Will's mum goodbye like an emu pecking a fence post, but she didn't seem to mind. I think Will's mum had enough bounce and cheeriness for the whole family.

'Sorry, Jim Wimple, love,' she said, nodding at Mr Maggot, who was scoffing my toast on his way out. 'He's got to get to work. There's cold pizza in the fridge?'

Will and I headed to school. Fiona didn't have to leave so early now she had a Bazoom! but it was probably a good thing because I needed to talk to Will about the night before. I explained my second failed attempt at leaving the Letter of Persuasion.

'So, let me get this straight. You went back to Mallet & Mullet a second time, but you *still* didn't manage to leave the note?' Will said.

'It was impossible,' I explained. 'I got completely lost and ended up in this weird room with these weird people who didn't seem to know who my dad was at first, and then said he was "the natural guy", whatever that means.'

'Well, he is quite natural,' Will pondered. 'I always feel comfortable in his company.'

'So do I, Will. But it's a weird thing to say, don't you think? In fact, the whole place is weird. I've started a new project to document the strangeness.'

'Well, you know what I say?' Will said boldly. 'Things are only strange until the truth is in range.'

'Which means?'

'Which means finding out the truth is important. The unknown is a scary thing.'

You're not kidding. Dad's late night 'at work' and his nifty trainers were playing on my mind. But I kept this to myself – too much information always distracted Will, and right now he needed to keep his eyes on the prize.

'More importantly we need to get that Bazoom! in range,' I said, yanking him into a side street.

I'd spotted Jeremy Flowers on the other side of the road. He was walking slowly and stopping every couple of metres to see how far ahead of him he could spit. I knew from experience that if Jeremy Flowers was in a spitting mood, you seriously didn't want to be within spitting distance.

'Your house after school,' Will said. 'Tonight's the night we bag the Bazoom!!'

'Yes,' I agreed. 'Tonight's the night we bag the Bazoom!.'

And, I decided, tonight was the night I'd find out what Dad was really up to. Forget Hettymail, this was pure curiosity – a burning question. So fiercely burning it felt like my brain was on fire.

After school that afternoon Will and I were settling down in my room to do some serious thinking (and munching on crisps I'd managed to smuggle in) when we were interrupted by a shriek. It sounded like a small animal in pain – or a beginner violinist, I thought, remembering Dad's joke. Will and I rushed into Hetty's room. Mum was there holding out a plate of brown lumps that clearly weren't wanted. Hetty had dressed for battle and was wearing a onesie, oven gloves and a cycling helmet, which wobbled as she shook her head violently in protest.

'Come on, Hetty,' Mum coaxed, 'You can't expect to grow tall if you don't eat your parsnip cookies.'

'Parsnips grow downwards,' Will said. 'They're root vegetables.'

'I don't want to be a root vegetable!' Hetty shouted.

'Heather, will you please just try one,' Mum said crossly. 'They're nutritious.'

'If I have one, I need to have a chocolate one after, okay?' Hetty bargained.

'Sorry, angel, we don't have any chocolate biscuits,' Mum said.

'Yes, we –'

I caught Hetty's eye and shook my head. If we gave away Dad's stash of chocolate biscuits we'd be in real trouble. *Later*, I mouthed. Hetty nodded minutely.

'Okay, then,' she said, taking a parsnip cookie. 'You can go now, shop's closed.'

Mum smiled with satisfaction. Will took a parsnip cookie from the plate as she left.

'Are you mad?' I asked.

'Just getting the truth in range,' Will said, taking a bite. He spat it out. 'Okay, I now know the truth.'

There was an almighty crash as Hetty tipped a box of toys onto the floor.

'What did you do that for?' I asked.

'I want to play Supermarket Shop. I need to find the shop stuff.'

'You'd find things a lot easier if you didn't make such a mess,' I tutted.

'It's not a mess, it's a filing system,' Will said, tilting his head to the side to see Hetty's bedroom from a different angle. 'All the important stuff stays on top of the piles and the less important stuff goes to the bottom. It makes perfect sense. If you don't play with your shop stuff very often, it'll probably be at the bottom.'

Will plunged his hand to the bottom of a pile of toys and brought up a bag.

'Wow,' Hetty gasped in total awe. 'My shopping stuff!' she said, wrapping her arms around him. 'Shop is open! What would you like to buy? Everything costs two p. Real two ps though, not plastic ones.'

'I'll buy something,' said a voice at the door. 'How much are hugs?'

'Daddy!' Hetty grinned. Then, more business-like, she announced: 'Hugs are five p.'

'So . . .' Dad began, rummaging in his pocket for five pence, 'chap at work said a boy came in last night looking for me.' Dad turned his head towards me.

'Wasn't me,' I said, shrugging. Dad frowned.

'It can't have been Jim. He was playing Blood Hospital with me all night,' Hetty said confidently. 'Do you want to know the details? They're a bit bloody. There was a lot of blood.'

Dad swayed slightly and shook his head. Hetty was one hell of a clever cookie – and a triple chocolate one at that. She gave Dad a huge hug and charged him ten pence. Then I got one, for free.

'So who do you think it was, Dad?' I ventured.

'No idea.'

'Perhaps it was a joke,' suggested Will helpfully. 'Accountants are always joking around.'

Dad shook his head. 'Very strange,' he said. 'Well, never mind.'

When he left, Hetty turned round and looked at us both in turn.

'You owe me,' she said.

As Will and I went back to my room I admitted I was feeling a bit shaky.

'I don't know why you didn't just tell him the truth,' Will said, climbing onto my top bunk. 'You were just a kid visiting his dad at work.'

'Sneaking out of the house late at night without even telling Mum? I don't think he'd believe I was "just visiting".'

'Well, you could just tell him about the Letter of Persuasion. I mean, he seems in quite a good mood now and he might be impressed by your dedication,' Will said, peeling off glow stars from the ceiling.

Will had a point. It's just the sort of thing

Dad would be impressed by – or so I once thought. But I didn't really know who Dad was any more, did I? And if 'Jim Supreme' hadn't worked, then there was no guarantee that 'Jim of Impressive Dedication' would either. I couldn't take the risk.

'We need to stick to the plan. If I rush it, there might be another NO.'

'No, you're right,' Will nodded.

'Mind you, Will,' I said, having a light-bulb moment, 'if he said NO twice that would be two negatives. Two negatives could make a positive!'

'Not in the art of flipping,' said Will, carefully resticking the glow stars. 'And if it gets as far as a NO-NO, flipping one wouldn't be enough, because then it would be a YES-NO and that's basically a MAYBE. MAYBEs are tricky. They're usually NOs in disguise. It has to be a simple flip – one NO to one YES.'

'I've got a feeling our chances to flip anything are running out,' I sighed.

'We've got to hit your dad with the double-hook then,' Will grunted as he stuck another glow star on the ceiling. 'Pathos and logos at the same time. You can't just beg, you have to reason with him too. We need to write a new letter. One that we actually deliver this time, one that says it *makes sense* to buy Jim Wimple a Bazoom!.'

So we wrote:

Dear Dad,
I have been your son for some time. I
have kept my room tidy and I've never
asked for a hamster, even though most
kids ask for a hamster or a bearded-
dragon or whatever every single day of
their lives. What I would really like is a

new scooter. There is a new one in the
shops called a Bazoom! and it's brilliant.
It has room for two people so I could
even take you for a ride on it. It also has
a boost function which gives you extra
speed, so I'll never be late for school.
Ever. I could also lend it to you when you
go trainspotting. You're allowed scooters
on train platforms – I checked. So you'd
never miss spotting another train.

Your son,

Jim

Will and I high-fived. He was certain this was
a winner. I certainly hoped so, although for me
it was only half the battle. I still needed to find
out what secret Dad was keeping from us. But
I had a plan – and this time we were going to
be in the right place at the right time, not only

to secure the Bazoom! but also to rumble the suspicious behaviour at Mallet & Mullet.

'To make sure we don't fail, the Letter of Persuasion needs to go somewhere everyone will see it, right?' I said. 'The more people the better. His office is hopeless. But remember what Dad's boss said on the phone – they're having a meeting tomorrow night at seven p.m.! Let's leave it in the boardroom where all Dad's colleagues will see it too. Better still, Dad's boss will be there. And who wouldn't want to look good in front of the chief? It'll have maximum effect. Dad's sure to buy me a Bazoom!.'

'For a boy with an average-sized head, your brain is quite big,' Will said, grinning.

'Well, you're hardly soft in the head,' I said, wanting to return the compliment.

'I am actually – we all are. Brain consistency

is jelly-like, you see,' Will said. 'If you called me Jelly Brain I'd be quite pleased.'

'By the way, nice glow-star arrangement, Jelly Brain,' I said. 'What is it?'

'A new constellation –' Will started. But just then Mum shouted up that Fiona was here to take Will (and his Jelly Brain) home for tea.

Fiona is often sent to collect Will even though he doesn't live far. It's to make sure he doesn't get sidetracked on the way home (following snail trails, usually). She looked pretty unhappy about it. I think it's because her mum said she had to give him a ride back on her Bazoom!. I felt a bolt of jealousy tear through me. More than anywhere in the world there are two places I wanted to be:

1. at the front of a Bazoom! driving, or
2. at the back of a Bazoom! holding onto
   Fiona.

Her hair was down, most of it covering her face. One ice-green eye peered at me through the fringe. She didn't come in. She just stood on the doorstep flipping a coin.

'What are you flipping a coin for?' I asked, trying to build a conversation while Will got his shoes on.

'To find out whether it lands on heads or tails,' she said in a bored voice.

'What happens if it lands on tails?'

'Tails I kick Will in the backside,' she said without smiling.

'Oh right,' I said, 'and if it's heads?'

'Heads I kick Will in the backside.'

Which got me thinking that maybe flipping something over wouldn't necessarily change the outcome. A NO might always be a NO, like a trick, double-headed coin. I shoved that thought to the back of my head.

'Are you Fiona?' asked Hetty, appearing at my elbow.

'Yes I am,' Fiona replied, her face softening at Hetty's cuteness.

'Jim wants to know –'

'If your friend got her Bazoom!?' I interrupted, pushing Hetty behind me.

'Yes,' Fiona answered, her face no longer soft. And that was that.

Will hopped onto the Bazoom! behind his sister. His mean, bossy, arrogant, amazing, beautiful sister . . . In my mind I saw myself performing a breathtaking trick on my red Bazoom! as Fiona watched in wide-eyed awe, dimples blazing.

Hetty watched them go, too, and stroked my arm.

'I wasn't really going to tell her, Jimble-wimble. But play shops with me now, or next time I will,' she bargained, with a twinkle in her eye and a quick punch to my ribs.

Chapter 9

Thursday arrived, and there had been a Bazoom! rush. The counter in Scoots showed '3 LEFT'. If Will's number theories were correct, this would very soon be two. With only three (two) Bazoom!s left, Will and I were certainly cutting it fine. But we had one really good shot at this, and even if it meant I was left with the last Bazoom! in the shop – which I suspected would be my least favourite colour, purple – it would be better than nothing at all. Because if this plan didn't work, that's what I'd have: zero Bazoom!, zero chance to impress Fiona and, most importantly, zero idea of what my dad was really up to. Operation Bazoom! and Operation Dad were now cemented together. And I had my project book and pen ready in my rucksack in case one gave me clues to the other.

The pavement outside Scoots was writhing with evening shoppers but Will and I were statue-still, eyes locked on the window display. The last three scooters were lined up – red, blue and purple. A big cardboard sign in front of them shouted 'Will It Be You?'.

'It's a sign,' Will said.

'I know that,' I said. 'I have eyes.'

'No, it's a *sign*,' Will repeated mysteriously. 'You could say: will it be you? Or, you *could* say: WILL, it be *YOU*! . . . As in me, Will Maggot. And it will, Jim. It will be me. When I say "me", I mean "us", though.'

I'd never seen Will so transfixed by the Bazoom! before.

Earlier that day Jeremy had threatened to steal Maximus (Will brought him to school for a project once) – but it was more than that. Will's ride home on Fiona's Bazoom! had been some kind of awakening. He had never shown any interest in anything fast before, but within minutes of looking into Scoots he'd done three speeding 'neeeow' sounds under his breath, and I could swear he was drooling over the blue one in the window.

Will looked at me with a face of sheer determination. It wasn't a look I'd seen before.

'Did you copy that look from your action movie?' I asked.

'Yes,' he replied, grinning. 'Does it suit me?'

'Well, it suits you better than *that*,' I said, noticing that under his jacket Will was wearing a baggy gold jumpsuit. He held out his arms.

'What's wrong with it?'

'It's a gold jumpsuit!' I said. 'What's *right* with it?'

'It's camouflage,' he replied stroppily, 'in case we need to hide on the carpet of your dad's office. Mum bought it for a 1970s fancy dress party.'

'Thank goodness for that, Will. For a moment I thought it was yours.'

Will went bright red. 'Well, she said I could keep it . . .'

'Right,' I said quickly, to cover his embarrassment. 'Come on, it's ten to seven. We've got ten minutes to get in and out of the Boardroom. We need to run!'

Inside the foyer of Mallet & Mullet we hid behind a large vase of lilies while we caught our breath.

'You know what I'm thinking?' Will said, panting, his hands on his knees.

'What?'

'I'm thinking about that film I watched. The boy gets past these baddies sleeping on the boat. But when I took the ferry to France there were always people walking around and buying chips or being sick. There was always someone awake.'

'It's a film, Will,' I explained. 'It's a made-up story. The people are all actors. It's pretend.'

Will went quiet. 'But this isn't pretend,' he said ominously.

'No, this is a real mission. Come on –'

Will pulled me back and I knew where this was going. Reality was hitting Will faster than a catapulted peanut at terminal velocity.

'But I'm not an actor!' he squeaked, looking at me, his eyes the size of avocados. 'I can't do this!'

'Of course you can, Will,' I said soothingly. 'With a jelly brain like yours you can do anything. You've rescued snails from furious campfires, rolled down steep hills . . . You once caught a cricket ball between your knees, remember?'

'I rolled because Fiona pushed me and that cricket thing was a fluke,' Will reminded me, but he was looking less avocado-eyed. 'The snail thing's true.'

'Precisely,' I said. 'You're a real-life hero. And we're just putting a letter on a table, we're not exposing a gang of dark villains.'

Will did some extra panting and then stood up straight. He nodded.

'Let's do it!' he said, although a little less macho than before.

We triggered Mount Fuji (which had moved again) and tiptoed down the gloomy, grotty corridor that turned one way, then another, none of it familiar even though this was now my third trip to Mallet & Mullet. Finally, at the end of a straight long corridor I saw the door we were looking for – *the Boardroom*. I tugged at Will's jumpsuit.

'Let's go,' I said, hurrying towards the Boardroom as quietly as I could.

The room was empty but laid out ready for the meeting. There was a large oval table filled with coffee cups, pens and paper. Will pointed to the papers on the desk and did a hand signal (I don't know . . . a caterpillar?).

'Let's just leave the letter and go,' Will whispered.

'No, let's hide,' I said. 'We want to hear the reaction when he reads the letter, don't we? And we're bound to discover something about Dad's work at the meeting, too.'

'Oh, for your project book,' Will said meanly, as if it was my new imposter best friend. 'What about the Bazoom! – or don't you care any more?'

'Of course I care. But I also want to know why my dad has a list of old people on his wall and weird machines in his room. Come on, let's be detectives.'

'Detectives are made-up people, remember?' Will sulked.

This was worth arguing about, but we didn't have time. 'Come on. When it's all over we'll laugh about it over a game of Mollusc Top Trumps.' Then I knew I'd won him over.

I fumbled in my rucksack for the Letter of

Persuasion but outside there was a sudden noise, like a fast-approaching swarm of bumble bees. It was the sound of lots of conversations at once.

The doorknob rattled. There was no time to plant the letter – we had to hide right away!

I pulled Will under the table and put my fingers to my lips. People came in, sat down and shuffled their feet under the table where we were hiding. Three pairs of nifty trainers came to rest just centimetres away from me. I looked over at Will, who was retying a pair of laces that had come undone. On someone else's shoes. I made a signal (furious badger?) and thankfully he stopped before they noticed anything.

Then a voice I recognised began to speak. It was the man from the creepy phone call – Dad's boss.

'*Evening, ladies and gentlemen. We have a lot to discuss, so we'll take plenty of short breaks to freshen up and stretch our legs. Right. First . . . Why don't we go to you, Mr Reaper? What have you got to report?*'

I heard someone cough as if they were about to make a speech.

'Evening, ladies and gentlemen . . .' they began. It was Dad! But why was he answering to 'Mr Reaper'?

'. . . and Mr Sinister. We've done rather well

this quarter,' he continued. 'No terrible mistakes to report, just a few trouble clients that have been making things awkward these last couple of weeks – in particular Arthur Mackles, Audrey Finnigan, Elsa McDougal and Penelope Dean. It would make sense to wait for winter before dealing with them because of course during winter numbers naturally increase. The cold season is a perfect time for absorbing extras into the register.'

What were they talking about? I'd heard of the tax year, but what on earth was 'the cold season'? Unfortunately for me, Mr Sinister wasn't giving Dad any time to explain.

'The case of Audrey Finnigan in particular has been a problem for too long, Reaper. So I think you should put that case in order as soon as possible before –'

'Certainly,' Dad interrupted. 'I will personally see to that this evening.'

Will yawned. I nudged him in the ribs.

'*Thank you, Mr Reaper. And while we're talking about the register, shall we discuss the possibility of upgrading our systems? It's been suggested we "get with the programme".*' There was laughter. '*So who here thinks we should invest in some computers?*'

I heard Dad laugh.

'In my opinion there's nothing wrong with our traditional methods, Mr Sinister,' Dad said. 'Indeed we find it keeps us more organised. And besides, we wouldn't want to risk any crashes or viruses. We have enough trouble avoiding those as it is! Hats off to Misadventures.'

There was raucous laughter. I didn't get the joke, but it sounded like a good one. So Will was right about accountants and jokes, if they *were* accountants . . . They didn't really sound like they were. A phone rang and Mr Sinister answered, saying 'yes' every couple of seconds.

'Okay, everyone. Something's come up, so let's take a short break and then perhaps when we get back Mr Black could give us his autumn report.'

Everyone got out of their chairs. Two people tripped (their shoelaces had been tied together), but eventually all the feet moved to the far end of the table. I heard the rattle of cups and requests for coffee, tea and shortbread biscuits. From under the table we watched feet swivel this way and that way as their owners chatted and waited in turn for tea and coffee. A biscuit fell to the floor and before I could stop him, Will scrambled forward and grabbed it. I did a furious hand signal that could possibly look like a lemming falling off a cliff, but Will understood what it meant. He nodded and jammed his hands into his armpits. No more biscuit snatching.

When I thought it was safe I crept closer to the edge of the table to take a look. Everyone was occupied at the other end and it looked as if I might be able to reach my hand up and place the Letter of Persuasion on top. But two pairs of long legs appeared at our end of the table, forcing me to duck back under. I peered up carefully. It was Dad and a tall man with long white sideburns. From the sound of his voice it was Mr Sinister, the boss. Mr Sinister must have been talking about the blood promotion, because I could just about see Dad's hands, and they were clenched so tight his knuckles were white. Then he started wiping his hands on his knees, leaving sweaty patches. Yep, they were talking about blood all right. Dad's legs suddenly turned and he ran for the door. If they'd been discussing BLOOD my bet was that he rushed to the toilet. Mr Sinister sighed and walked back towards the 'refreshments' end of the table.

Now was the perfect moment to leave the letter . . . I unfolded it but my hand was shaking. Really shaking. Suddenly I didn't feel confident about any of this – what if Dad's lovely colleagues weren't lovely? What if Dad felt humiliated in front of them? What if we were discovered and Mr Sinister sacked Dad? Panic rose in my throat, making me feel very odd. I needed air, I needed to escape. We had to get out and get out now, before the nifty trainers circled us once again. We could form another plan later. I signalled Will to follow me, and he did. Quickly and quietly we crawled out from under the table and scampered on all fours out of the Boardroom. I took a last look before we crawled round the corner – no one was looking. We'd made it!

'For funny accountants, that was pretty boring!' Will exclaimed once we were back in the corridor.

'Yes . . .' I agreed, although I didn't agree at all. I'd been suspicious about Mallet & Mullet, but now I knew for certain that something wasn't right. Dad's accountancy job simply didn't add up. And that's exactly what accountants were supposed to do: add up.

'You didn't leave the letter,' Will noted.

'I know, I know. I have another plan,' I said. I didn't. But I did have questions. 'Will, why do you think they said numbers go up in the cold season?'

We stood up and Will rustled as he shook out the creases in his gold jumpsuit. 'I don't know. I guess it's a bit like a numerical mating season.'

'But numbers don't mate.'

'Many things don't mate, Jim. Like the hammerhead shark and some forms of fungi. They just multiply if the conditions are right. Perhaps numbers multiply when it's cold.'

I usually try not to laugh at Will because it's not his fault there's no filter between his brain and his mouth and, like I said, occasionally there's a bit of brilliance in his messy mind. But this time I couldn't help myself – it was probably nerves. I laughed. I laughed and laughed . . . I couldn't stop myself and I reached out my hand to Will to say sorry, knowing he'd be upset, but when I looked up he wasn't there.

'Will?'

'Shhhh.'

'Will?'

'I'm over here,' he whispered.

He'd dropped to the floor and rolled down the corridor and was beautifully camouflaged on the golden carpet, apart from his eyes which were blinking at me furiously. He grimaced and did something with his hands (a nervous hamster?) but when that didn't work, he just pointed.

'You can get off the floor now,' Dad said, calmly, looking down at Will.

Chapter 10

Dad had a strange look on his face.

'Dad . . .'

'Were you in the Boardroom?' he asked quickly.

'No,' I lied. 'We just arrived.'

Dad looked a bit relieved by this. Then he peered curiously at Will's jumpsuit.

'And *why* are you here?'

'We were looking for you,' I said. 'We got, er, lost.'

'We came about the scooter,' Will said, shrugging me an apology.

'What scooter?' Dad asked, looking at me. I was red, I knew. My cheeks felt hot.

'Jim wrote you a letter all about it,' Will said. 'We came to deliver it. Would you like to read it now?'

'Yes, yes. Let's get out of here and then you can tell me all about it,' Dad said, looking up and down the corridor cautiously. 'Why don't we go to my office?'

We walked in silence down corridors that twisted this way and that, my dad behind us, his hands on our shoulders. Will and I slowed down when we saw the G. *Reaper* door but he gently pushed us further on, back towards the foyer, back past the spooky portraits.

'Nice picture, Dad. Not sure about your

friends – especially the one at the end with the bone necklace. Is he the inventor of accounting?'

'Yes, yes. Just a joke,' said Dad.

Will nudged me. 'Told you accountants were funny,' he said.

Dad opened the door (I saw him nudge the last portrait on the wall) and we re-entered the blinding white of the modern foyer.

'By the way, how did you get in?' Dad asked, as casually as he could, steering us to the other side of the foyer, away from where we'd come, away from Mount Fuji.

'Doors were open,' I smiled.

'Very strange,' he murmured.

He pulled a small black box from his pocket, pointed it at the wall to the right of the exit where there was a patch of wall space with no pictures. He pressed a button and the wall parted to reveal a little room. 'Right,' he said. 'Here we are, this is my office.'

This office had hard black-and-white chairs and a large wooden desk and a modern telephone and a computer and bookshelves stacked with accountancy law volumes, numbered one to one hundred. On the walls were charts and pictures of people shaking hands and looking pleased with themselves, and a photo of Dad with some writing underneath: *Terry Wimple, Senior Accountant, Mallet & Mullet.*

Dad sat down with a big whoosh on his leather swivel chair on the other side of the desk and put on a big, broad smile. But I knew Dad's smile – I knew it inside out and back to front. Dad smiled a lot, especially when watching Mr Bean. Every time he knew Mr Bean was about to do something rude or ridiculous, his mouth stretched wider and wider and his eyes twinkled and his cheeks bobbed up like bouncy apricots. That was Dad's smile. What I saw was *not* Dad's smile. It was sudden and thin-lipped. His eyes didn't twinkle at all.

'Come and sit down,' he said, gesturing to the black-and-white swivel chairs.

'Is that your computer?' I asked, stupidly relieved to see one.

'Certainly is,' he said, giving the machine a pat. 'Let me just . . .' Dad started tapping at the keyboard – 'finish this email . . . There!'

He certainly looked like an accountant when he was tapping at the computer.

'So, Dad –' I began, but he held up his finger to say 'hang on a minute' and picked up the phone.

'Ah, Susan. I have guests. Could you bring in

two lemonades . . . And bring in the files on the, er, Fitzpatrick account . . . Oh, and –' he said this very quietly, '– I'm in the front office.'

Dad placed his hands on the table. 'So tell me about this scooter,' he said.

'It's all in here!' said Will. 'You were supposed to read it in front of everyone, but, well, never mind . . .'

He handed over the letter as Dad chuckled. But I knew Dad's chuckle inside out and back to front – like when he watched Mr Bean pour oysters into a woman's handbag, it was a low gurgle that grew into a giggle that exploded into cackles. This was *not* Dad's chuckle. It was a low ha-ha-ha, as if he were about to sneeze, not laugh. He read the letter through and sat back deep in thought. *Bazoom!*, he mouthed, *Bazoom!* . . .

There was a quick knock at the door and a

woman we recognised as the secretary came in with two lemonades and a bundle of papers, which she lay on the desk and patted. 'Your accounts work,' she said with snappy efficiency, giving us another glimpse of her chipped front tooth before she walked out, leaving the door open.

'So, this scooter . . .' Dad began, but some people from the meeting had appeared in the foyer outside. They were milling around, untangling their shoelaces and talking loudly. 'Damn door,' said Dad. 'Susan!' he called angrily.

Dad's annoyed voice matched his tense face far better than the smile or the chuckle had. Something was wrong. Very wrong. Will was spinning in his chair, but my head was spinning all on its own. Everything in this front office looked right, but the truth still didn't seem in range. I was starting to feel sick.

'Susan!' Dad shouted again. Then he got up to shut the door himself. Fired by curiosity I pulled his paperwork towards me – there was nothing there! Just empty, blank pages. I swung the computer screen round. It was switched off! *What was going on?*

Dad walked back to the desk, adjusting his fake smile. 'So, where were we?' he said.

'It's really not important,' I said hurriedly. 'Come on, Will. We need to go, don't we?' I grabbed his jumpsuit and began tugging at it so he would get up. 'We promised to meet your sister, didn't we?'

'No . . .' Will said.

'Yes we did,' I insisted, giving him a punch on the arm.

'Ow!'

'Yes, NOW. That's right, Will,' I said, dragging him to the door. 'See you at home, okay, Dad?'

'Read the letter again,' Will called as we opened the door. 'Sleep on it! Maybe just a quick nap though – we're running out of time.'

I gave Will's arm a yank and finally we rushed outside. I turned round to see Dad in the doorway, watching us go. I wish we'd both worn dark blue this time, but Will was in a gold jumpsuit and I was wearing a Christmas present from Mum – a luminous T-shirt saying *Veg Of Glory*.

Will and I stopped for a breather round the corner outside Scoots. Eventually Will turned to me and smiled.

'I think that went quite well,' he said.

'I'm not sure it did,' I said, hardly caring. I was feeling all mixed up and queasy. Will did moon eyes at me and stuffed his hands in his pockets.

'I'm sorry I rushed the Letter of Persuasion

without asking you,' he said, twisting his body side to side. 'I was feeling kind of desperate. See, I've got kind of obsessed. With Bazoom!s. I even asked my mum for one.'

'You asked your mum for a Bazoom!' I repeated.

'She said no, and lots of other things, too. Totally unflippable. So when we didn't get a chance to leave the letter – again – I just panicked. Sorry. Sorry, Jim.'

'Doesn't matter, Will,' I said. I just wanted him to stop talking so I could think. But Will was animated.

'But I think it turned out okay. I mean, he was totally up for being persuaded. He got us lemonade! I reckon he'll go out straight away and buy a –' Will turned to the Bazoom! display in the window behind us. The digi-counter said '1 LEFT' and it was blinking, too, just to rub it in. *One left, one left, one left . . .*

The bright red one in the window – my favourite, now decorated with balloons – was the last Bazoom! in town. Will gasped for air and flapped his hands.

'Jim, your dad needs to be down here first thing in the morning to get the final Bazoom!.' I didn't respond. 'Jim, it's Friday tomorrow. Someone will get Friday fever and buy it, I know they will! Fridays are like that.' My mind was blank. 'Jim, Jim, Jim . . .' He did a star jump to get my attention. Some passers-by laughed.

'Will, I need some time on my own. I'll follow you in a minute.'

'Okay, okay,' Will said soothingly, more to himself than me. 'Don't worry. I'll think of something.'

'Oh, and Will?' I said, as he mounted his scooter.

'Yes?'

'Find out what you can about Audrey Finnigan.'

'She owns three parrots.'

'Yes. Try to find out more than what you already know. And do it fast.'

'Okay, Jim.'

I didn't scoot home. Instead I went back to where we'd just come from. I leaned against the outside wall of Mallet & Mullet, took my project book out of my rucksack and jotted down some thoughts:

1. 'Dealing with trouble clients' – *does this mean making deals?*

2. Front office – *pretend office? Cover-up?*

3. Dad's personality different at work . . .

It became clear that the more I wrote, the less I knew about Dad. The only thing I was certain of was this: he was not a regular accountant called Terry Wimple. He was 'G. Reaper'. I didn't even know what the G stood for: Gary, Graham, Gerry . . . Goodfella? And if he had a fake name, then I had to assume he had a fake job, too . . . And the only reason you would use a false name and a false job was if . . .

I paused to wonder if what I was about to write was just plain crazy. There'd be no harm in jotting it down though, would there? My hand shook as I put the pen to the paper . . .

4. Mallet & Mullet – not accountants but *CRIMINALS*!

A man wearing a black cloak and very nifty trainers emerged from the building. I flattened myself against the wall and scribbled:

5. Black cloaks – *to hide guns?*
6. Nifty trainers – *to creep up on people?*

The man looked left then right before stepping out into the night. I knew that man. Walking and tiptoeing with action-movie stealth, scooter folded under my arm, I followed Dad across the road and down the high street. I ducked in and out of doorways and hid behind bus stops with my mind on staying unseen and keeping hot on his trail. I tried not to think of what to say if he caught me following him, or what I'd do if I caught him red-handed being a criminal, handing over burglars' maps of Buckingham

Palace or handling illegal shipments like the baddies in Will's action film.

To my amazement he headed back towards Scoots. He slowed down and peered through the window and I hid behind a rubbish bin to watch. The shop was dark but the window display was lit up like the best party in town, its last, bright red Bazoom! positioned centre stage. Balloons, flashing lights and streamers were hanging from the handlebars – it looked incredible. Dad must have thought so too because he stared at it for a long time. Was he imagining what it would be like if he surprised me with a Bazoom!? Was he picturing my face, struggling to contain an enormous smile? Was he seeing the two of us, riding it together, whooping and cheering as we popped the boost button and sped towards the train station? Well, me too. Me too. Although my imagination included an extra bit about Fiona (but I'm too embarrassed to mention it now).

Dad then got a piece of paper out of his pocket and read it. The Letter of Persuasion!

Yes! The Bazoom!, that's the one, Dad! Yes, yes, yes! . . .

Dad pulled a face – a sad 'not this time, kiddo' kind of face – and he shook his head a little. He crumpled up the letter and threw it in the bin I was hiding behind. I heard the paper ball plummet into rejection oblivion. My heart plummeted with it. What? The Bazoom! wasn't going to be mine after all, after *everything* Will and I had been through, after *everything* we'd tried? . . .

My eyes stung, my throat throbbed and my feet felt as if they were made of rock. I was tired, hungry and gargantuanly disappointed. But I had to pull myself together.

Operation Bazoom! might have flopped but Operation Dad wasn't over. And if I gave up my investigation I would never get the truth in range. Dad and his work would always be 'strange'. And nobody wants strangers in their family. I fought back tears and ran to catch up with Dad. He was on the move again, heading towards the multistorey car park. The car! I'd have to get in it too or I'd lose him. I felt sweat tingle behind my ears.

I matched Dad's footsteps, placing each foot down at the same time as his on the echoey car-park floor. I couldn't risk creating any extra noise. The neon lighting made strange shadows on the walls and I kept well hidden behind the rows of pillars. Dad pressed a button on his key ring and the car peeped twice as it unlocked. Our car was an estate car with a large boot compartment connected to the inside. If I could just get to the boot I could hide in it quite well. But how was I going to do that without him spotting me?

Dad was taking big strides. Three more and he'd be in the car and driving away. I had to distract him. There was an old metal hubcap leaning against a pillar. I grabbed it and rolled it hard down a concrete ramp to the side of us. It rattled and scratched and whirred loudly as it picked up speed, and Dad stopped, startled by the sound. Just as I'd hoped, he went to investigate, jogging down the ramp to see what was causing the commotion, and in a flash I was tucked up in the boot compartment, squeezed between the small side window and a bumper box of lentils.

Dad returned and I felt the jolt of the car as he sat in the driver's seat. Then he switched on the radio and – singing loudly to 'I Like to

Move It Move It' – drove out into the night.

But we weren't going home.

We stopped and Dad got out. I lifted my head and peered out of the side window, but it was dark and I couldn't make anything out, just shadowy doorways. I pushed the lentils aside and scrambled to the opposite side of the boot compartment. There was a dim street lamp on this side of the car, and through the other side window I could just about read the street name (I made a mental note) and I could also see Dad. He was walking up the driveway of number forty-seven. He didn't knock. He gently pushed open the front door and went inside. I faced a dilemma. If I followed him I could be caught or left behind. But if I stayed in the boot of the car, what would I learn?

I was searching for a coin to flip when the decision was taken out of my hands. Dad was getting back into the car and we were off again. We stopped at a few more streets and a few more houses, where Dad did the same in-and-out thing, and I wrote what I could in my project book – road names and house numbers. Then we stopped at a house in Will's road. *It must be Audrey Finnigan, the troublesome client!* She had three parrots. But what else? A stash of guns? A suitcase of stolen money? The floor plans to the Tower of London?

Dad took longer this time and if I'd known, maybe I'd have followed him. He came out of Audrey Finnigan's house after three, maybe four, minutes, wiping his brow. He sank heavily into his car seat, like a man exhausted. What torture had that woman put him through? Did she have 'heavies' in there with her – men with mean faces, big muscles and flick knives in their belts? Perhaps she had threatened that he would swim with the fishes if Dad didn't steal her the crown jewels.

I peered above the back-row seats and studied his face in the rear-view mirror. His eyes were shut, he was catching his breath. How could all this agony be worth it? It seemed an awful lot of stress to go through every day just to provide for his family. And if he took the promotion – the blood money – it would only get worse . . . He'd be tired and sick all of the time. I felt desperate and my mouth was dryer than one of Mum's chickpea muffins. I needed to tell Dad that I was on his side. I needed to tell him that he didn't *have* to do this job. I had other ideas – he could be a children's entertainer or a lollipop man or a teacher (not a maths teacher). But how would I tell him? How would I find the words?

Dad's eyes sprang open and I dropped back

down behind the seats. He put on his favourite song – 'Groove is in the Heart' – and sang all the way home. He was trying to make himself feel better. That song always cheered him up.

Dad went into the house. I followed a minute later, tiptoeing past the kitchen, where he and Mum were talking. I sat at the top of the stairs, listening to the murmur of voices below. He was telling Mum about me, Will and the Bazoom! – I could tell by her gasps.

'Bosoms?' she asked loudly. 'Why bosoms all of a sudden?'

I let Dad put her straight and crept into bed. Both of them came up to see me but I kept my eyes squeezed tight and pretend-snored until they left me alone. I didn't want to answer any questions.

I had too many of my own.

Chapter 11

The following morning I got up early and left the house before the rest of my family woke up. I waited at the end of Will's road, eating chocolate biscuits I'd pinched from Dad's stash, until Will eventually turned up. He was wearing glasses.

'You don't wear glasses, Will,' I commented.

'I do now,' he said. 'I've decided that there is always too much to see. But if I frame what's in front of me, my brain will be more efficient.

It's a long-term experiment. You should expect to see me wearing these for quite a while.'

Fiona tore up the road towards us on her Bazoom!. We asked if we could hop on the back but she sneered at us and scooted off with a shout of, 'No chance, losers!' She even did a pop-boost jump off the pavement (awesome).

'I rang Scoots first thing this morning,' Will said, turning to me. 'They'll hold the last one for us.' He was definitely on a mission.

'But it's only eight thirty, Will. They're not open yet.'

'I left a message on their answerphone. A very *persuasive* message.'

'It's no good, Will.' I sighed.

'It bloody well is!' he said, crossly. 'I used a philosophical argument, and if I tried my philosophical argument on you I think you'd find –'

'Will,' I said gently. 'I'm sure your message was great. But it's no good because my dad has said NO again. A final NO. That's a NO-NO. It's non-flippable.'

'But – but . . . how? When? Why?'

'I followed him last night. He went to Scoots, looked at the Bazoom! and he shook his head.'

'Probably had a spider on his head,' Will said, shaking his own head furiously.

'No spider.'

'The wind tickled his ears.'

'I don't think so.'

'Maybe he was just thinking, *"I wish they'd made scooters like that in my day."*.'

'It was a NO. I know my dad.'

That bit was a lie as it turned out because I didn't really know Dad, did I? But I did know a NO when I saw it.

'Oh . . .' Will put his face in his hands.

'But there's something else – I'm worried about Dad. I think he's caught up with dangerous people.'

Will was upset about the Bazoom! but he's a really good friend and good friends can see when you need help. So he told me to tell him everything, the full story. I got out my project book from my bag and showed him, going through all the absurd details: unanswered questions about cloaks and nifty trainers, my theories about criminal gangs and high-prize burglaries, the late-night visits to make money deals with trouble clients . . . His eyes grew wider and wider like slowly inflating beach balls.

'But I still don't get the promotion with blood,' I said.

'Blood money is when you pay people to keep quiet when you've killed someone,' Will said quietly. 'It was in the action movie. Oh hula hoops, Jim! What are you going to do?'

'I'm going to take my evidence to Dad,' I said, pulling myself together. 'And first you're going to help me collect it. So start by telling me what you found out about Audrey Finnigan.'

'Oh yes!' Will said, suddenly animated. 'I remembered, Jim! I did find out some stuff. I spoke to Mum yesterday and apparently Audrey Finnigan is eighty-seven years old and she's got three parrots.'

'Anything else?'

'She grows runner beans in her back garden. Um . . . she also grows rhubarb and gooseberries.'

'Apart from fruit and vegetables . . . Anything else?' I tried very hard not to look impatient.

'No . . . ' Will shook his head. 'Oh, actually, yes, there is one thing.'

'What?'

'She died.'

'WHAT?'

'Ambulance was here at six o'clock this morning. We all stood out in the street in our pyjamas. The paramedic woman said she'd died.'

'Will, come with me,' I said, pulling at him, goosebumps galloping up my arms.

'But we'll miss school . . .'

'Yes, but this is more important. I think Dad is being framed!'

'For another portrait?'

'No, Will – for murder.'

We took a map from the Tourist Office, found a bench in the park and spread it out. I highlighted the roads Dad had driven to the night before.

'Okay, so these are the places Dad stopped

off. You take the ones on the east side and I'll take the ones on the west side. Find out as much as you can about the people in those houses. Let's meet at Shakalaka Milkshake bar in an hour's time.'

Will nodded, and that's all he did, which gave me some hope that he understood the serious nature of our investigation. This wasn't a harmless interest in what my dad did for a living any more. This was a matter of life and death.

On my scooter I revisited the roads Dad and I had been to the night before, and one by one I ticked them off while a big knot of anxiety grew in my stomach: Washington Terrace – ambulance; Mulberry Mews – no answer; Caroll Street – 'with sympathy' flowers on the doorstep; Flinders Lane – ambulance . . .

When I met Will at Shakalaka Milkshake bar

he was looking equally queasy. I felt bad that I'd involved him now, as he's very sensitive. I gave his shoulder a squeeze.

'Are you okay, Will?' I said tenderly, and he shook his head.

'I'm never ordering vanilla shake with three syrups again,' he said. 'Blurgh.'

'Oh, right. And what did you find out?'

'Nothing,' Will said, taking another slurp of his revolting milkshake. 'No one answered any of the doors, and there was a police car blocking one of the roads. Sorry.'

'Don't worry, Will. It's just as I feared,' I said sadly. 'They're all dead.'

Will whipped off his glasses. 'You don't think your dad took the blood money promotion, do you? You don't think he killed them?'

'My dad is scared of blood, remember?' I said. 'He couldn't kill a mosquito without falling into a coma. But he's caught up in something very bad. I've been thinking about how it all works, and here's what I've come up with: I think Mallet & Mullet is an organisation that trades secrets – villains pay them for top-secret information.'

'Like what?'

'Like the names of rich people, the plans to Buckingham Palace, maps of underground tunnels for smuggling, top secrets . . .'

'Blackmail!' Will joined in. 'That's a low-down crime, that is.'

I gulped. 'Yes, maybe. And I think Dad's working for some of London's most devious low-down crime lords – Dad's "trouble clients"! They're trouble with a capital T. Crime lords always have enemies – *other* crime lords. I think Dad's clients are being knocked off by a rival gang. The gang strikes right after Dad's visited so the police will think it's him! Like I said, he's being framed! Come on, we need to go to Mallet & Mullet. We need to tell Dad he's in terrible danger.'

We ran through big glass doors, and although there were people in the foyer – possibly *dangerous* people – we didn't hang around. Will and I rushed straight past them and swung Mount Fuji. The people behind us shouted *STOP!* but we didn't. The walls slid open and we ran down the corridors, knocking dusty portraits sideways and bumping into Mallet & Mullet workers, sending eyebrows flying in alarm and papers flapping in the air. There were more shouts of *OI!* and *STOP!* and *RING THE ALARM!* but we didn't stop running until we reached the door saying *G. Reaper*.

We burst through the door. Dad jumped out of his skin.

'What the –?' he screeched.

'Hi Dad,' I panted, apologetically. 'Didn't mean to alarm you.'

Dad looked worried and he had a reason to be – there were people out to get him. Any moment there would be police surrounding the building, preparing to arrest him and put him behind bars.

'Jim –' Dad began, but his office door swung open again and Susan with the chipped front tooth stepped in, balancing a pot of coffee and a plate of biscuits on a tray. She was looking down, being very careful not to spill anything.

'Morning, Grim –' she said before looking up and stopping abruptly. She placed the tray on the desk and left quickly, like a startled mouse.

'Morning *glorious* actually,' Will said, seriously. 'Trouble is you've got no windows in here so you wouldn't know. It's actually one of those nice crisp autumn days with blue sky . . .'

Will tailed off when he saw Dad's face. It was long and pinched – a bit like his portrait on the wall of accountants. It's a look I would come to call the Cold Eye.

'Now look here,' Dad started, but I held up my hand to stop him.

'Dad, we know everything,' I said. The colour drained from his face and I knew my worst fears were right.

'How did you know?' he asked.

'Well, it started with your offices and everyone acting strangely, and then there was the stuff at the meeting – yes, I lied, we were there, hiding under the table – and your weird

working hours and those "trouble clients" . . .
Be honest, Dad . . .'

I paused for effect. Dad wrung his hands.
Will picked his nose.

'. . . You're working for criminals – trading
secrets like Hetty does but worse, much worse.
You're caught up in a cyclone of lies, theft and
violence, aren't you?'

Dad remained totally still with his eyebrows
bunched together. His eyes wandered aimlessly.
He was thinking. Something wasn't right.

'Dad, this is serious. I know you're a good
man. But now you're being framed for murder,'
I continued. 'The trouble clients you visited last
night – they're all dead!'

'Are they?' he said in a surprised kind of
voice.

But I knew Dad's surprise inside out and back
to front – when Mr Bean's funny little car was

run over by an army tank, he leapt to his feet and put his hand on his heart and said 'goodness!' in a high-pitched voice. And right now he wasn't surprised at all . . . He *knew* they were dead.

I felt a cold shiver run down my spine.

Perhaps Dad wasn't *in* trouble – maybe he *was* trouble.

My brain went crazy and I suddenly remembered the killer cone snail Will once told me about. Lovely looking thing, but if you step on it you're dead meat.

'You're not working for criminals,' I said, the words catching in my throat. 'You're the boss, aren't you? A crime lord. The man at the top . . .'

Dad shook his head.

'So you're a spy, then? A double agent? A bounty hunter?' I was becoming desperate.

Dad held up a hand, sighed and shook his head. 'I am not working for criminals and I am not a criminal boss or a secret agent or a bounty hunter.'

I knew Dad's truths inside out and back to front. This was one of them, at last. He met my eye and nodded to reassure me. He wasn't lying.

'You promise?' I asked fiercely.

'I promise.'

'On your life, my life, Hetty's life and Mum's life?' I challenged.

'I promise. I promise on life itself,' he said, placing his hand on his heart.

'Then what is this all about?' I said in a squeak. 'You have no computers, you run around in nifty trainers, you work weird hours . . . What *do* you do?'

Dad dragged one hand down his face like a flannel and scratched his chin.

'You just wouldn't understand,' he said finally.

'I would –' I started, but he shook his head.

'You should leave now.'

There was something in his voice that told me I shouldn't push it any more, and anyway, my brain was tired and my head was aching and my heart was feeling stretched and sore. I felt like I'd run cross-country for miles. Dad accompanied us down the old corridor, with its peculiar pictures and wooden doors and old telephones, nudged the last portrait on the wall and led us out into the foyer. He put a hand on each of our shoulders.

'I'll see you at home later, Jim. Now get back to school, both of you.'

He disappeared back behind the sliding doors. I was shaking.

'You need to sit down,' Will said tenderly.

We sat together on a slippery leather sofa

under the Eiffel Tower. I found myself sobbing a little bit.

'I don't get it,' I mumbled snottily. 'I just don't get it. I thought I had a normal dad with a normal job and now I know that's not true. But even after all our detective work, that's still all I know. The truth isn't in range, Will. Everything's still strange, and my dad is a stranger. If I'd discovered he was a poison-dart shooting ninja, it would have been better than this. Because at least I'd know the truth!'

Will rubbed my arm. 'I know,' he said with a big sigh. 'It's frustrating. All our investigating . . . all those clues . . .' He adjusted his glasses and stared ahead. 'We just have to face it – we've come to a dead end.'

I nodded. But then I looked up.

'What did you say?'

'I said, "All our investigating –"'

'No, the last bit.'

'We've come to a dead end.'

'Say it again, Will. Say it again.'

'Dead end. This is a dead end.'

Chapter 12

We ran back down the corridors, our hearts racing, armed with a mind-blowing theory. *G. Reaper* wasn't in his office. But startled chipped-tooth Susan was and she told us where to find him. He was in the General Office – the one at the end of the corridor that had machines and loud number-shouting (we wouldn't be falling for that again!). I opened the door and peeked through, unnoticed, watching as Dad ran his finger over a large map of London and his co-workers punched buttons into the big metal machine. They were all wearing black cloaks and there was a neat row of white trainers along the wall . . .

'Come on,' I said to Will.

'If you're sure,' he nodded.

'One, two, three!'

We flung open the door and I gave a little cough to show we were there and suddenly – like programmed puppets – they all jumped up and grabbed telephones and talked about accounts and stuff. Dad froze. His face looked thunderous. But I had adrenalin pumping through my veins – I wasn't scared.

'You can stop pretending to be accountants!' I said loudly.

The workers just called out numbers even louder.

'What's three hundred and sixty-five divided by five?' I shouted.

The room went silent.

'No? Well what about four times fifteen?'

The workers blushed.

'You can't even do simple maths!'

'To be fair,' Will whispered, 'you've given them some tricky ones.'

There was not a single calculator in sight. Not one high-tech computer. Not even an abacus. But that didn't matter, because they weren't accountants. None of them were.

'Four times fifteen is thirty . . . maybe?' said a nervous man at the back of the room.

Dad held up his hand. 'Okay, stop. Go ahead, Jim, talk.'

So right there, in front of everyone, I presented our theory. Well, it was *my* theory. Back in the foyer under the Eiffel Tower Will said it was bonkers but he'd back me up because that's what best friends do. And it was bonkers – but it was the only explanation . . .

Dad didn't move an inch the whole time I was speaking, but the other workers left one by one, tiptoeing like naughty kids trying to sneak out of a maths test. That was good – I wanted Dad to be on his own when I accused him of the most awful, vile, wicked crimes to humankind.

'. . . And don't say I have a good imagination, Dad,' I said sternly when I'd finished. 'I know I'm right.' I stamped my foot for emphasis. Will stamped his, too. It echoed in the silence.

'You're right,' Dad said calmly, shoulders slumping.

'Pardon?'

'You're right,' he repeated.

'But – but – it can't be. It's impossible!' I cried, my voice shrill.

'Make up your mind, Jim,' Will moaned.

'You're the GRIM REAPER?!'

'Only at work,' Dad replied. 'At home I'm still Terry –'

'How can it be?' I shouted. 'You're my dad. You live with me. You like *Mr Bean*! You can't be a killer! . . .'

'I'm not a killer,' Dad said calmly. 'I'm in charge of natural deaths in Greater London. I only work with very old people. I take the ones who are ready to go.'

'Sounds reasonable,' Will nodded, obviously untouched by any sense of reality.

I pulled up a chair and sat down heavily.

'So you're not an accountant . . .' I said, a bit stupidly.

'Well, no, I'm terrible at maths, Jim. A snail would do a better job.'

'Everything's connected,' Will whispered wisely.

'And who are all the other people at Mallet & Mullet?' I asked.

'Mallet & Mullet is a cover-up. It's actually The Dead End Office, Jim. Some people here deliver messages, work the machines, provide the names of clients – you know . . . people who are leaving us. And some are my helpers. For when it gets busy.'

'In the cold season,' Will added knowingly.

'And the nifty trainers?' I asked. 'What are they for?'

'For when we need to do things as quickly as possible.'

'What things?' I asked.

'I'm not telling you the procedure, Jim. It's confidential.'

'But what about the trouble clients? Like Audrey Finnigan? Did you *murder* her?!'

'Audrey Finnigan's time was up a long time ago but she had been taking some medicines that interfered with the process. The medicines were only making things worse. It was important that I took her before her illness became unbearable. Before she was taken in a less dignified way. I like to keep things natural if I can.'

'Definitely a natural guy,' Will noted.

'And what was the promotion about – with blood?' I asked.

Dad turned pale. 'Um,' he gulped, 'I was

asked if I wanted to take over . . . Misadventures.'

'What's that?'

'Misadventures is like the special forces of death. They swoop in as quickly as possible to take people involved in accidents and disasters – those in pain. It's a noble job, but it inevitably does involve b-b-b—'

'I hope you said no,' I said quickly, seeing Dad go wobbly at the thought of it.

'I said no,' Dad hiccupped, holding the back of his hand to his mouth.

'Just no?' Will asked. 'Got to watch that – if you only say no, it can easily be flipped.'

Dad looked confused.

I explained: 'Will said we could flip your NO into a YES – you know, about the scooter I wanted.' Dad nodded but didn't say anything.

'Maybe you'd like to get one for me now? There's one left . . .' I tried.

It was cheeky but worth a shot, and actually I felt like I really did deserve one – you know, after discovering that death was what my dad handled for a living . . . Will did little gleeful jumps on the spot. Dad held up his hand again.

'When you first mentioned the Bazoom! it rang a bell,' Dad said quietly. It was the sort of quietly that makes you listen. 'A month ago I overhead someone from Misadventures telling Mr Sinister – that's my overseer, my boss – how they feared a new turboscooter might soon be responsible for some . . . endings,' he said tactfully. 'They research this kind of thing all the time. The safety of the Bazoom! is in question. I'm afraid the Bazoom! may be doomed. And you are definitely not going to be a candidate for an early ending, son,' he said, stroking my cheek tenderly. 'Not while I'm in town.'

We were all silent for a while. I was trying to get to grips with everything (Will might have been thinking about the density of a cheese sandwich – you could never tell) and I'm sure Dad was wondering what to do now we knew that he wasn't an accountant, but DEATH – not Terry Wimple but THE GRIM REAPER.

'Does Mum know?' I asked, momentarily horrified that she was Death's Wife!

'Yes. She's always known . . . We've been protecting you, Jim,' he said. 'And now I think it's time we forgot about it.' He smiled sadly.

'What do you mean?' I asked.

'I'm going to erase your memory. It's for the best.'

'No!' I shouted. 'You can't do that!'

'I can,' Dad said. I looked at Will, who blinked furiously behind his glasses.

'Look,' I said hurriedly. 'If you erase my memory then this will all just happen again. I have a really active curiosity. One day I'll want to find out what you do, and this will happen over and over and over. We'll keep a secret. No one will ever know. You're my Dad. I won't let you down.'

'Yeah,' Will said helpfully.

Dad thought for a while and nodded. Will and I looked at each other with relief.

Then Dad took my hand and wrapped his fingers round it. He looked at me and smiled.

He gripped tightly.

A weird atmosphere took hold of the room, as if a wind had come through and cleaned the air. Dad kept squeezing my hand and I kept on squeezing back as if we were caught in an invisible tornado and my life depended on it. After moments, the air settled and he let go.

'He won't remember anything about these offices once you're outside,' Dad said, pointing to Will, who was looking dazed. 'Nothing about this place or my work.'

'How did you do it?' I gulped.

'Brain training,' Dad said. 'And I'll say no more.'

When we were outside I told Will that we'd skived school to check out the Bazoom! situation at Scoots and he didn't question it. So that was okay. But as I looked behind me, at Dad standing in the foyer, my stomach lurched.

The Grim Reaper, Death – AKA my dad – gave me a wave and disappeared back into The Dead End Office.

Chapter 13

I came home full of nerves. Mum met me at the door and offered me a KitKat, which was weird because I know from her that chocolate and sugar aren't 'part of a healthy diet'. Dad must have phoned to tell her the news. Hetty came downstairs when I shut the door and stared at the KitKat in my hand until I snapped a piece off for her. Usually I'd resist sharing such a rare treat, but I was glad she was there. It meant we couldn't talk about Dad. I didn't want to talk about him, you see – I mean, what would I say? *Hey Mum, so Dad's a spooky guy! . . . Hey Mum, how do you sleep at night?*

'What's that on the ceiling of your room?' Hetty asked.

'What were you doing in my room?'

'Tell me what it is,' she demanded. 'Then I've got something to tell *you*.'

'It's a new constellation Will created.'

'Looks like a snail.'

'It probably is,' I smiled. Of course it was.

'What have snails got to do with stars?' she snorted. 'Stars are bright and amazing. Snails are ordinary. They hide in their shells when you poke them.' She poked me in the ribs. 'But you can get them out with a fork,' she said, grinning wickedly. 'The French think they're delicious.'

I thought of my ordinary dad and how I'd

eventually forced him out of his shell with my fork of determination. But the result hadn't been delicious – it had left a bad taste in my mouth.

'The whole world is connected, Hetty,' I said, wanting to defend Will. 'Anyway, what were you going to tell me?'

'I went for a play-date with Kimmy Flowers today.' She nibbled the edge of her KitKat nonchalantly.

'Jeremy Flowers' sister?' I gasped.

'Yup. And I found out some *very* interesting information, just for you.'

Hetty stood on tiptoes and whispered in my ear and I couldn't believe what she told me! Stories of Jeremy's 'cuddle blankets' and how his mum has to kiss each of his toes every night before he goes to sleep – and how he's scared of carrots!

'Is all this true?'

Hetty nodded victoriously. 'If you threaten to tell the whole school, I don't think he'll bully you and Will any more.' She winked and looked past me, over my head. 'Daddy!'

I couldn't help it, I tensed up. Dad was looking a little nervous too, but he ruffled my hair and told Hetty another skeleton joke he'd heard at work and he kissed Mum and asked about business at The Happy Husk and said he was

Starvin' Marvin' and was there any leftover dinner he could have. He looked normal. His eyes twinkled and his mouth smiled, but still, everything was different now. When he looked at me my heart skipped wildly and my skin tingled with fear. I didn't mean to but when Dad came near me I shrunk back like a poked snail. Just before bed he asked me if I fancied a game of Connect Four but I said I was tired and went to my room.

There I lay on my top bunk, hoping my heart would calm down. With my eyes closed I tried to think of positive things like the weekend ahead, what flavour crisps I'd buy from Streets on Tuesday and whether I should be more adventurous and buy a packet of Brain-Sparks. Which reminded me of Will's jelly brain. Wiped clean of memory. And what about my own? After today it would be quivering with new information. I was surprised it hadn't gone into shock. Or maybe it had. Maybe this is what shock felt like. I couldn't sleep, even after Hetty had come in and kissed every one of my toes goodnight for a giggle.

It was late. On the landing I could hear Hetty whistle-snoring from behind her bedroom door. I crept downstairs and looked in the living room at Mum and Dad. They were fighting over the television controls.

'But there's the final of *The Great Cake Bake* on,' Mum said, snatching it from Dad.

'But I want to watch *Great Trains of the Twentieth Century*,' Dad grunted, pulling it back.

'If you let me watch *The Great Cake Bake* I'll make you something with chocolate in it,' Mum pleaded.

'Proper chocolate? I don't want any chocolate courgette brownie nonsense . . .'

'Ooh you cheeky . . .' Mum prodded him, and he tickled her back. 'Terry, stop it!' she laughed.

They both laughed. Then Dad sighed – a big, loud, public sigh. He slipped his arm around Mum's shoulder and stroked her hair.

'Do you think Jim's okay?' he said quietly.

'He just needs a bit of time,' Mum said softly.

'You don't think he hates me, do you?' Dad wiped something from underneath his eye.

'Of course not,' Mum protested. 'He'll be fine, he's just had a shock. Terry,' she said, giving him a big caring squeeze. 'You're his dad. You'll always be his dad.'

Suddenly everything was clear to me. It was like I'd put on Will's framing glasses and brought the important things into focus. If I stopped fretting over the mind-boggling details about life and death and nifty trainers, and looked at what was right in front of me, I would see Terry Wimple, AKA my dad, the nicest dad in the world. And he thought I hated him!

Of course I didn't hate him. I loved my dad more than anything. And if people had to be taken by death, then nobody could take them with more kindness than Dad. When it came to kindness, Dad was a natural.

'I'd better be off,' I heard him say.

'Again? What time will you be back?' Mum asked.

'As soon as I can, darling. As soon as I can.'

As he stood up to go I ran down the stairs

and wrapped my arms tightly round his waist. Dad's arms encircled me and he gave me a long suffocating hug. Neither of us pulled away and we stood there for ages, rocking from foot to foot, not wanting to let each other go.

After Dad had gone I went upstairs and opened my project book. I stared at it for a while, looking over all the facts and clues that had brought me to the door of Grim Reaper. Nothing was strange any more – the truth was in range. Okay, it was kind of a strange truth, a surprising truth, a truth that would make most people stick their fingers in their ears and shout, 'Not listening, not listening.' I had been like that at first, but not now. I mean, this was one of life's big questions – if not the biggest. There was so much to discover and I couldn't wait to ask Dad for all the details. Like what was the *Glove Room*, how did the machine work, and what did the flashing light bulbs mean on the wall?

But that was for another project book. This one had served its purpose. I wrote in it one last time.

Project finished.

Conclusion: Dad is Death.

Signed: ~~Jim Wimple.~~

Jim Reaper

Will would have loved all this, I thought. If he liked Curly Wurly bars because they illustrated the complexity of life, my revelations about The Dead End Office would be like a chocolate factory explosion. It would blow his mind! And I wished I could tell him that maybe he was right – about everything being connected – and about how holding Dad's hand had miraculously protected me against the memory wiping, just like snail touch-telepathy . . . But I could never tell him. I had promised Dad. I suddenly had the urge to call him, though, and find out if he was okay.

'All right, Jim?' Will answered. 'It's a bit late

in the northern hemisphere. Are you working on southern hemisphere time? Because if you are you really need to give people notice. Southern hemisphere is hours ahead.'

'Sorry, Will.'

'It's okay. Mum's having a disco down in the living room so I can't get to sleep anyway. What's up?'

'Nothing really. Just wanted to say hello.'

'Hello.'

'Hello. So how are you feeling?' I said.

'Bit annoyed, actually,' he said. 'The last Bazoom! has probably gone now.'

'Don't worry, Will. Jeremy Flowers won't be bothering us.'

'Why not?'

'While I was finding ways to get a Bazoom!, some details emerged. Details Jeremy wouldn't want anyone to know . . .'

'But how?'

'Let's just say everything's connected, Will. Everything's connected.'

'I'm glad you realise that,' he said with a satisfied voice. 'But I can't believe our combined genius failed. And now some lucky sod will be riding around on that red scooter – OUR RED SCOOTER, Jim!'

'Life's a bit unfair sometimes.'

'Dead right, it is,' Will said. 'Well, I hope he falls off and hurts his knee.'

'That's not very nice,' I laughed, surprised at Will's passion.

'I know,' Will said. 'Sorry. Mum's playing rap music. Rap music always makes me moody. I'll be nicer in the morning. I don't *really* want anyone to have an accident.'

The word rang in my ears. *Accident* . . . *Accident* . . . *Accident* . . .

ACCIDENT!!!

Suddenly, it came back to me – Misadventures' predictions about the Bazoom! . . . *Fiona had a Bazoom!*. If anything happened to Fiona I'd . . . I'd . . . I couldn't bear to think about it. We had to take away her Bazoom! – steal it, trash it, throw it in the river. ANYTHING!

'Will!' I shouted into the receiver. 'I'm coming over.'

'At this late northern hemisphere time?'

'Yes, Will, I'm coming over right now. There's something we've got to do.'

Will's mum shouted something in the background.

'I'm on the phone,' Will shouted back at her. 'It's just Jim Wimple.'

But I'm not just Jim Wimple, I thought to myself. *I am Jim Reaper, Son of Grim.*

I paused to smile at my secret name. Then I

pounced into action. Fiona was in danger and although she didn't know it, she needed my help.

It was time for a scram sandwich.

I repeat: it was time for a scram sandwich.

Acknowledgements

Special thanks to my friend and partner, Mike, for his patience and support, and to my wonderful parents for their unwavering belief and humour. Big inexhaustible thank yous to Alice Williams and Matilda Johnson. And to my eager readers Lizzie & Tom, Jerome, Elise, Ollie, Emile, Angus, Fleur, Lars and Sammy – I would buy you all Bazoom!s if I could. Shiny red ones.

Read on for the first chapter
of the next JIM REAPER book

JIM
REAPER
Saving Granny Maggot

'Hilarious and fun and spooky and brilliant!'
PAMELA BUTCHART

Rachel Delahaye
Illustrated by Jamie Littler

When I Told Will . . .

'Cool!'

I couldn't believe my ears.

'Perhaps you didn't hear me,' I said. 'I didn't say "I'm saving up for a skateboard" or "last night I saw a fox in my garden". I said "my dad is the Grim Reaper". Will, MY DAD IS DEATH!'

'That's so cool,' Will yelped, eyes like bagels.

'You don't think better words might be *weird* or *creepy*?'

'Coooool!' he said one more time, slowly. His mouth hung open like a broken snapdragon.

So, I had just dropped a bombshell – front-page news, the full enchilada, the biggest, maddest, most eye-stretching piece of information a boy could ever imagine: I live with Death. DEATH is MY DAD! And what did Will think?

He thought it was *cool*.

'What, Will? What's cool, *exactly*?' I was exasperated.

'What's out there and stuff, Jim. You know . . . How it's all connected.'

The whole world is connected is one of Will's sayings, and I tell you, he can find a link between anything – a Siberian hamster and a French baguette, a nose hair and a grain of rice. But my dad being Death and that being cool? Will's very own connection with reality was looking a bit shaky.

I snapped. 'Forget what's "out there". I'm talking about what's right here. Aren't you freaked out?'

The answer was no – Will wasn't the tiniest bit freaked out. 'So when does he go out and make people dead, then? Does he stalk the streets?'

'Of course not! He turns up when people are ready to die.'

'People call him? There's a hotline number?'

'No. He just pops round to their house and, er, makes them dead.'

'Urgh, that is horrid!' Will exclaimed, but there was a grin fixed from one ear to the other. I think he had Morbid Curiosity. It's when you're fascinated by death. I should know.

'So how does he actually do it? Is it like –' Will clutched his throat, pretending to strangle himself. 'Or how about –' He mimed stabbing himself in the heart.

I wondered if insanity was a side effect of morbid curiosity, because Will wasn't being very Will all of a sudden. My friend Will thinks *SpongeBob SquarePants* is an emotional roller-coaster, and he's not the type that likes blood, guts and violence. At a Romans dress-up day at school, we all came as centurions, naturally. Will came as a market fruit-seller.

Will put the imaginary knife into his heart and pulled it out again, laughing.

'Cool,' he said again, clutching his sides.

What I hadn't told him yet was that my dad, Death, was out to get Will's granny. Not cool. Not cool at all.

Chapter 1

But let's go back a bit. Back to when the world as I knew it changed forever. Back to when I found out that my dad was not Terry Wimple, Senior Accountant at Mallet & Mullet, but the Grim Reaper.

How did I find out? Let's just say that there were things about Dad being an accountant that didn't add up – including the fact that he's rubbish at maths. So if he wasn't an accountant, what was he? My investigations led me to his office, and what I saw there I'll never forget, unless Dad wipes my memory (I'll explain later). The Mallet & Mullet building was modern and shiny on the outside, but behind secret sliding doors there were fusty old corridors and ancient paintings and strange rooms – Brain Training rooms, Glove rooms, goodness-knows-what rooms and the General Office room. Things got super weird when I went in *there*. Offices normally have computers and printers and stuff, don't they? Well, there wasn't a computer to be seen. Not even a calculator. It was full of creaking machines and people dressed in black cloaks, who, when given a quick maths test, convinced me they weren't accountants either. None of them were. To cut a long story short, I confronted Dad with a theory. An impossible theory. He was Death. Only he went and admitted it!

So, there it is: Mallet & Mallet is a pretend accountancy company – a cover for The Dead End Office, where Deaths do their paperwork. And Dad and his team of Deaths are responsible for Natural Deaths in Greater London. They takes the oldies, basically.

When I discovered that, it should have been the end of the story. But it wasn't.

Usually my investigations, such as *My Roof: A Landing Pad for Aliens?*, have solid conclusions, like *No, the Patches on the Roof are Caused by Poor Insulation*. And then there's nothing much more to say (unless you want to talk about insulation. I don't). But this investigation was different. Knowing Dad's real job didn't provide me with a satisfying conclusion – it just made me want to know more. I had millions of questions, like *What is the Meaning of Death?* It made me want to jump in the deep end. Let me explain.

Some questions have a shallow end and a deep end, a bit like a swimming pool. You can touch the bottom easily with a simple answer, but if you're looking for a more complex answer you can quickly get out of your depth. It's one of Will's theories. He introduced it to me when I asked if he preferred roasted or salted peanuts. Will explained that the shallow-end answer was 'salted', but for a deep-end answer he'd need to ask more questions, like 'In what situation – extreme hunger or light snacking?' and 'Are there any other nut types on offer?' as well as 'How old are the nuts?' My best friend might act like he has marshmallow brains, but there are solid nuggets of biscuity brilliance inside Will Maggot's head. He's kind of shallow and deep, himself. Like a Wagon Wheel or a Tunnock's Teacake.

What does that have to do with *the Meaning of Death*? If you've done life cycles in your science lessons you'll know that death means there is no heartbeat or brain function. But that's just the shallow answer. Oh yes . . . Like Will's peanuts, the deep end of *What is the Meaning of Death?* is more complicated – it's a question made up of more questions, which I'll tell you in a minute. And I wanted the answers to those questions more than I wanted a lifetime supply of prawn cocktail crisps (which was quite a lot).

Of course, I asked Dad right away. After all, he was pretty much the expert on Death, and asking questions is what a healthy inquisitive kid is supposed to do. I said: 'Tell me more about death.' He said: 'I couldn't possibly burden you with the details, son,' and I said, 'Go on,' and he said, 'You should be living for the moment, not worrying about the end.' But I was worrying about the end – dying to know, in fact – so I fired the full list of deep-enders at him in one go:

What is the *meaning* of death?

How do you dead people?

Why do you dead people?

Do you *have* to dead people?

What happens if you *like* who
you're about to dead?

What would happen if you
refused to dead someone –

Actually, I didn't make it through the full list, because Dad stopped me. Not with one of our usual wordy jokes, like 'You're *dead* curious today, Jim' or 'You're making a *grave* mistake by asking me all these questions.' No. He stopped me with The Cold Eye.

My dad has a friendly face, like an old-fashioned policeman or a carol singer on a Christmas card. *So* friendly, you'd never expect it could look menacing or dangerous. But when Dad sucks in his cheeks and narrows his eyes, he can look surprisingly evil – like a vampire sucking a lemon. That, my friend, is The Cold Eye. Without saying a single word, The Cold Eye shouts, 'BACK OFF OR THERE'LL BE TROUBLE!'

The Cold Eye can't be ignored, so I did back off, quickly.

But the questions rattled around inside my brain, distracting me during the day and keeping me up at night. They were begging to be answered. And if Dad wouldn't give me the answers, I'd just have to go hunting for them. I picked a brand new project book off my shelf, unwrapped it, opened it, and wrote the title in bold letters:

What is the Meaning of Death?

I quite often use project books for my investigations. That's because if you write down everything you know (even stuff that seems irrelevant) you can sometimes fit it all together like a jigsaw and find the truth. It's what detectives do. *Nothing is strange when the truth is in range* – that's another one of Will's sayings, and it's one that makes a lot of sense (a lot of his really don't, at least not to me).

Let me show you what I wrote.

WHAT IS THE
MEANING OF DEATH?

Things I know about
The Dead End Office

Fact 1. Dad is in charge of Natural Deaths

Dad only does Natural Deaths. He takes away old people whose time is up.

Note: I don't know how he does it, but Dad says this is painless and I believe him, because he's a big softy.

Fact 2. The Misadventures Team

The Misadventures Team work at the scene of fatal accidents (unnatural deaths) to bring death quickly, so people don't suffer too much. They also take people who get really ill to stop their pain. And they help deal with Trouble Clients.

Note: Dad turned down a promotion to Misadventures because he's scared of blood.

Fact 3. Trouble Clients

Trouble Clients are people who Dad is having trouble getting rid of, and Dad's boss gets cross if there are too many of them.

Note: I think some medicines get in the way of the death process.

Question: Why are Trouble Clients a problem for The Dead End Office? (NB, see title of this investigation.)

Fact 4. Deaths wear Nifty Trainers
These trainers are designed for speed and silence, so Deaths can work quickly, undetected.
Note: They look quite comfortable, although I haven't tried any on yet.

Fact 5: Memory Wiping
Dad did special Brain Training and can wipe people's memories.
Note: I do not want this to happen to me – ever.

Conclusion: I do not have enough facts to form an opinion about the Meaning of Death.

Note: I need more facts.

Read all the
JIM REAPER books!

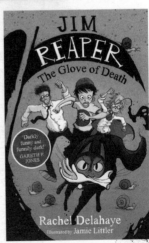